THE ADVENTURES OF BILLY BOLTS

GEARS OF FATE

To my wife of 14 years, Cristen. Happy Anniversary.

THE SPARK IGNITES

Melvin's pulse hammered in his ears as he gripped the control pad, thumbs dancing across the interface. Sweat trickled down his temple, catching in his three-day stubble. The crowd's roar faded to white noise as he focused on the towering metal behemoth he'd spent eighteen months building.

Sixty feet of gleaming titanium and carbon fiber, "The Peacekeeper" moved with surprising grace for something that weighed twenty-seven tons. Its hydraulics hissed as it dodged a plasma burst from the opposing machine —a monstrous construction called "Dreadnaught" with serrated blades for arms.

"Come on, baby," Melvin muttered, executing a sequence that sent Peacekeeper into a defensive crouch. The arena floor trembled beneath the impact of the massive machines.

Dreadnaught charged, its pilot going for a finishing move. Rookie mistake.

Melvin's fingers flew across the controls. Peacekeeper dropped lower, caught Dreadnaught mid-stride, and used the momentum to flip the enemy robot onto its back. The crash echoed through the arena like a bomb detonation. Before Dreadnaught could recover, Peacekeeper planted a massive foot on its chest plate and activated its primary weapon.

The electromagnetic pulse cannon hummed to life. One blast, and Dreadnaught's systems went dark.

The arena erupted. Holographic fireworks exploded overhead as the announcer's voice boomed: "PEACEKEEPER WINS! MELVIN APPLEBAUM TAKES THE CHAMPIONSHIP!"

Melvin exhaled for what felt like the first time in minutes. He pushed his welding goggles up onto his forehead and wiped his face with a rag. Victory felt good, but something nagged at him.

From his control booth, he glanced up at the VIP observation deck where Zoltar stood applauding. The old man's smile didn't reach his eyes.

"Congratulations, Mr. Applebaum." A sleek assistant appeared at Melvin's side. "Mr. Zoltar requests your presence at the winners' reception. He's particularly impressed with your EMP technology."

Melvin nodded, but unease settled in his gut. He'd noticed Zoltar's scientists taking unusual interest in his designs during preliminary inspections. The questions they'd asked went beyond standard tournament protocols.

"I'll be there," Melvin said, watching as technicians swarmed his robot below. One of them was scanning Peacekeeper's weapon systems with an unauthorized device.

Something wasn't right. Nobody had seen last year's champion since the awards ceremony. Or the year before that.

Melvin slipped through the shadows of his laboratory, the cold glow of monitors painting his face in harsh blues. Massive machines loomed around him like silent sentinels. His fingers trembled as he activated a small recording device.

"If you're watching this, I've disappeared." He glanced nervously at the door. "Zoltar's tournament isn't what it seems. The winners don't retire to private islands. They vanish."

He pulled a maintenance panel from a knee-high utility droid—R4, his first successful build from engineering school. The bot chirped questioningly.

"Easy, buddy." Melvin patted its dome. "Need you to hold onto something important."

He slid the data chip into a hidden compartment beneath R4's secondary processing unit and sealed it with trembling hands.

"Find the Temple of the Node. The Order will know what to do with this information." Melvin's voice dropped to a whisper. "Zoltar's building something. Something terrible."

A crash echoed from the front of the building. R4 whirred in alarm.

"Go! Back exit! Now!" Melvin shoved the droid toward the rear of the lab.

Heavy footsteps approached. Melvin grabbed a wrench, backing against his workbench as the door burst open. Three figures in sleek black armor stormed in, weapons raised. Behind them stood one of Zoltar's white-coated scientists.

"Mr. Applebaum," the scientist said, adjusting his glasses. "Your presence is required at the main facility."

"I declined the invitation," Melvin growled, glancing at the window where R4 had just disappeared.

"It wasn't an invitation."

A sharp pain bloomed in Melvin's neck. He slapped at it, fingers finding a small dart. The room tilted sideways as his knees buckled.

"Your EMP technology is... revolutionary," the scientist's voice echoed strangely as darkness crept into Melvin's vision. "Mr. Zoltar has plans for you."

Melvin's last conscious thought was of R4 speeding away through the night, carrying the only evidence of what he'd discovered about the tournament, about Zoltar, about the missing engineers.

Then blackness swallowed him whole.

Melvin awoke to the sterile gleam of chrome and glass. His head throbbed with each pulse of the ambient lighting that rippled across the obsidian floors. He tried to move, but restraints held his wrists and ankles to a reclined chair that felt more medical than comfortable.

"Our champion rises." Zoltar's voice carried across the room before the man himself appeared, shuffling forward with the whir and click of mechanical supports. His frail body was a stark contrast to the technological marvels that kept him mobile.

"Where am I?" Melvin's throat felt raw, his words scraping out.

"The winners' circle." Zoltar's smile stretched thin across his face. "Though perhaps not the one advertised in our brochures."

Melvin tugged against his restraints. "You've been kidnapping engineers."

"Recruiting." Zoltar corrected, circling Melvin's chair. "The finest minds deserve the finest facilities. Your EMP technology is particularly impressive. Non-lethal but devastatingly effective." He leaned closer, his breath smelling of artificial mint. "Imagine it scaled up. Imagine entire cities going dark at the push of a button."

"That's not what I built it for."

"Creators rarely envision the true potential of their work." Zoltar gestured expansively. A wall panel slid away, revealing a window that overlooked an enormous laboratory. Below, dozens of engineers worked at various stations, surrounded by robot parts and weapon prototypes. "Welcome to my underground labyrinth, Mr. Applebaum. Your new home."

Melvin recognized faces from past tournaments—champions who had vanished from public view. Now they worked like automatons, their movements mechanical, eyes vacant.

"What have you done to them?"

"Compliance chips." Zoltar tapped his own temple. "Most required... persuasion. Some came willingly after seeing the scope of our operation." He pressed a button on his wrist device, and Melvin's restraints retracted. "You'll join them in The Forge. Your EMP technology will be the cornerstone of my new offensive systems."

"And if I refuse?"

Zoltar's façade of pleasantness evaporated. "Then you'll work without the luxury of free will." His eyes narrowed. "Your little droid—R4, was it? My retrieval team is tracking it as we speak."

Melvin's blood ran cold. If they caught R4 before it reached the Temple...

CHAPTER 2: ECHOES IN THE RAIN

Twelve years later, Billy "Bolts" Applebaum hunched over a battered workbench in his garage, fingers dancing across the innards of a defunct service droid. Rain pattered against the corrugated roof, providing a soothing backdrop to the quiet hum of his soldering iron.

"If I bypass the security protocol..." he muttered, pushing his welding goggles up onto his forehead to get a better look at the delicate circuitry. "Then cross-wire the auxiliary power to the main processor..."

The droid's eyes flickered with a weak blue light.

"C'mon, you can do it," Billy coaxed, adjusting a final connection.

The light steadied, then brightened. The droid's head swiveled toward him with a mechanical whir.

"System reboot complete. Awaiting instructions."

Billy pumped his fist. "Yes! That's seven for seven this week." He made a note in his already-full repair journal, the margins crowded with technical sketches and improvement ideas.

At thirteen, Billy towered over most kids his age, his stocky frame and serious expression often causing strangers to mistake him for someone much older. It was an illusion that shattered the moment he got excited about robotics, his hazel eyes lighting up with childlike enthusiasm.

He glanced at the clock—2:17 AM. No wonder the house was silent. Mom would be furious if she knew he was still up, but nights were when Billy felt most alive. When the world went quiet, he could hear the machines speak to him in their own language of clicks, whirs, and binary logic.

The repaired droid tottered across his workbench, executing a series of diagnostic movements.

"Functional enough for the scrapyard," Billy sighed. "But nothing special."

He'd salvaged it from behind Megaton Electronics last week. The thirteenth droid he'd rescued this month. Thirteen—like his age. A coincidence that felt appropriate for a kid with few friends beyond the mechanical companions he brought back to life.

Billy's room overflowed with salvaged tech and half-finished inventions. His classmates called him weird for preferring the company of machines to people. They didn't understand that droids were predictable, fixable. People were messy, complicated, and often cruel to anyone different.

He picked up a framed photo from his desk—his father, Melvin, standing proudly beside a combat robot prototype. The only memory Billy had of the father who'd disappeared before he was born.

Billy grabbed his worn leather engineer's jacket and slipped out through his bedroom window. The night air in Biome Synthesis's Southern District carried the distinct smell of rust and decay beneath the engineered foliage. Unlike the gleaming central rings with their self-sustaining ecosystems and living architecture, the outermost southern edge where Billy lived was the city's forgotten appendage.

Here, the grand ecological experiment faltered. Genetically modified plants struggled against pollution from nearby industrial zones. Buildings were conventional structures retrofitted with half-hearted biometric systems that frequently malfunctioned. The canals ran murky, and the solar collectors were outdated models that barely captured enough energy to power the district's basic needs.

But what the Southern District lacked in ecological harmony, it made up for in mechanical treasures. Billy navigated familiar alleyways, his steel-toed boots splashing through puddles reflecting the dim bioluminescent streetlights. He headed toward his favorite hunting ground—the unofficial scrap heap that had formed behind the district's recycling center.

"Hey, Bolts!" called a gruff voice as Billy passed a modified living wall where vines grew around salvaged machine parts. Old Man Jenkins, the neighborhood's nocturnal gardener, waved a soil-covered mechanical hand—his own creation after losing his real one in an industrial accident. "Hunting for treasures again?"

"Always," Billy replied with a grin. "The recycling center got a shipment from the Central Hub yesterday."

"Lucky you. Found a moisture regulator myself. Might get these vines to actually produce oxygen now."

Billy continued on, passing ramshackle homes where residents had ingeniously integrated discarded tech with the city's biological systems. A family had rigged old cleaning bots to tend their algae farm. Another used salvaged cooling units to maintain a small medicinal garden.

In the Southern District, survival meant reimagining

waste. While the inner rings of Biome Synthesis showcased humanity's ecological achievements, the outer ring demonstrated human resilience. Here, among the city's forgotten, Billy felt at home. Every discarded servo motor or cracked neural processor was potential waiting to be unlocked.

The scrap heap came into view, a mountain of mechanical parts glistening in the moonlight. Billy's playground. His classroom. His future.

Billy climbed the uneven slope of the scrap heap, his tool belt jingling with each step. He'd organized it meticulously—voltage testers on the left, precision screwdrivers center, and his prized magnetic retrieval tool on the right. The night's haul looked promising. A shipment from the Central Hub always meant high-quality castoffs.

He spotted a servo arm from an environmental maintenance droid, still in decent condition. As he reached for it, voices carried from the other side of the heap.

"Thought I heard something. Probably just Bolts the Bot-boy," came a familiar sneer.

Darius Chen and his crew. Billy froze, crouching lower behind a gutted cleaning unit.

"That freak's probably out here making himself a daddy," Darius laughed. "Since his real one didn't want him."

The other boys snickered. Billy's fingers curled around a rusted gear, squeezing until the edges bit into his palm.

"My dad says his old man was some kind of robot fanatic who ran off," another voice added. "Like father, like son, I guess."

"Nah, I heard his dad was actually a robot. Only explanation for why Bolts is such a weirdo."

More laughter. Billy closed his eyes, his chest tight. The usual mockery, but it never stung less.

"Hey Applebaum!" Darius shouted into the darkness. "Your mom ever tell you why your dad left? Was it 'cause you were already such a disappointment as a baby?"

Billy stood, unable to help himself. "At least my inventions work, Chen. Unlike that solar glider you crashed at the science fair."

Five boys emerged from behind a pile of discarded drones, Darius at the center, his sleek Central Hub clothing marking him as an outsider slumming it in the Southern District.

"Look who crawled out of his cave," Darius smirked. "The fatherless freak of Southern District."

"Don't you have some plants to water in your fancy inner-ring house?" Billy shot back.

"Just checking out where the desperate people live." Darius picked up a broken circuit board and tossed it at Billy's feet. "Making friends with garbage because no one else will talk to you?"

"These parts have more potential than you ever will," Billy said, his voice steady despite the burning in his throat.

"Potential for what? To be trash? Like you?" Darius laughed. "No wonder your dad bailed."

Billy turned his back on Darius and his crew, descending the other side of the scrap heap. Their taunts faded as he put distance between them, his tool belt clinking with each determined step.

"Idiots," he muttered, wiping at his eyes with his sleeve. "They wouldn't recognize innovation if it bit them on their—"

A small sniffling sound stopped him. In the shadow of a discarded refrigeration unit sat a girl no older than seven, cradling something in her arms. Tears streaked her dirt-smudged face.

"Hey," Billy said, approaching cautiously. "You okay?"

The girl looked up, startled. When she saw Billy's size, she shrank back.

"It's alright," he said, crouching down to appear less intimidating. "I'm not gonna hurt you. What's wrong?"

She hesitantly held out what she'd been cradling—a small companion bot, roughly the size of a kitten. Its metallic surface was dented, one eye-light flickering weakly.

"Mimi won't wake up," the girl whispered. "She's my friend."

Billy recognized the model—a basic companion droid designed for children in the Southern District who couldn't afford the advanced biometric pets popular in the inner rings.

"Mind if I take a look?" he asked, already reaching for his diagnostic tool.

The girl nodded, carefully transferring the small bot to Billy's hands. He ran his fingers over the dented chassis, finding the access panel.

"What's your name?" he asked as he worked.

"Ellie."

"I'm Billy. But some people call me Bolts." He popped open the panel, revealing tangled wires and a power core that had slipped from its housing. "What happened to Mimi?"

"My brother got mad and threw her against the wall," Ellie said, voice barely audible. "Mom says we can't afford a new one."

Billy nodded, understanding completely. In the Southern District, even basic companion bots represented months of saving.

"Good news," he said, reaching for his precision tools.

"Mimi's just sleeping. Her power core got knocked loose, and there's a crossed wire. I can fix her right up."

Ellie's eyes widened. "Really? How much will it cost? I have three credits saved..."

Billy waved her off. "No charge. Just watching out for a fellow robot friend."

His fingers worked deftly, reconnecting the power core and replacing a frayed wire with one from his belt pouch. He cleaned the optical sensors with a special cloth, then sealed the panel.

"Ready to say hello?" he asked, pressing the reboot switch. The little bot hummed to life, its eye-lights glowing bright blue. It chirped a happy greeting and swiveled toward Ellie.

"Mimi!" The girl scooped up the bot, which nuzzled against her cheek with a mechanical purr. "You fixed her!"

"Good as new," Billy smiled, packing away his tools. "Maybe even a little better. I boosted her battery efficiency."

Ellie threw her arms around Billy's neck, nearly knocking him backward. "Thank you, thank you!"

After Ellie left, clutching Mimi to her chest, Billy remained alone in the scrapyard. The encounter had left him with a familiar warmth—machines were simple to fix, their problems solvable with the right tools and knowledge. People, though? Their issues ran deeper, messier. Machines never mocked you for being different or abandoned you without explanation.

He kicked at a pile of discarded parts, sending a small avalanche of metal tumbling down the heap. Something glinted at the bottom of the newly exposed section—a dull silver casing partially buried under rusted gears and broken circuit boards.

"Hello, what's this?" Billy muttered, digging through the debris.

He uncovered what appeared to be a data storage unit, but unlike any standard model he'd seen before. Its design was elegant, almost military-grade, with reinforced corners and an unusual locking mechanism. No manufacturer's mark, no serial number—strange for any commercial tech.

Billy turned it over in his hands. The unit was heavy, suggesting serious internal hardware. A small panel on one side had an outdated connection port—at least fifteen years old based on the configuration.

"You're not from around here, are you?" he whispered to the device.

Something about it felt important. Significant. Billy slipped the unit into his jacket pocket and glanced around to ensure no one had seen his discovery. The last thing he needed was Darius and his crew demanding he hand over something potentially valuable.

The walk home was tense, his hand repeatedly checking his pocket to make sure the device was still there. Each time his fingers brushed against the cool metal, a strange excitement coursed through him. This wasn't just another broken bot to fix—this was something different.

Back in his room, Billy carefully placed the mysterious unit on his workbench. The cathedral of mechanical chaos around him suddenly felt like the perfect sanctuary for this strange artifact. He pulled his goggles down over his eyes and reached for his diagnostic tools.

"Let's see what secrets you're hiding," he murmured to the device, his isolation momentarily forgotten in the thrill of discovery.

CHAPTER 3: TRACES OF A GHOST

Billy had just connected his diagnostic pad to the mysterious data unit when three sharp knocks rattled his door.

"It's open," he called, not looking up from his work.

The door creaked open, and Cristen slipped into the room, expertly navigating the maze of parts on the floor without disturbing a single component.

"Hey, Billy." She tucked a strand of raven-black hair behind her ear. "Your mom said you brought home something interesting from the scrapyard."

Billy glanced up, momentarily startled. Cristen was one of the few people he actually enjoyed having in his space. Unlike others who saw only mess, she understood the method behind his mechanical madness.

"Yeah, check this out." He gestured toward the workbench where the data unit sat beside the robot he'd salvaged earlier. "Found both today."

Cristen's bright green eyes widened as she leaned over the bench. "Whoa, what model is that?" She pointed at the robot, its weathered frame propped against a stack of technical manuals.

"That's the thing—I don't know." Billy adjusted his welding goggles on his forehead. "No serial number, no manufacturer marks. The design is... different."

Cristen circled the workbench, studying the robot from all angles. She reached out, tracing her finger along an unusual joint in the machine's arm.

"The articulation points are military-grade," she observed. "But the casing looks civilian. It's like someone deliberately tried to make it look ordinary."

Billy nodded. "Exactly what I was thinking. And look at this." He pointed to a small compartment in the robot's chest. "Hidden storage, magnetically sealed. Whatever this bot was designed for, it wasn't just serving drinks or cleaning floors."

"Can you get it working?" Cristen asked, excitement dancing in her eyes.

"Maybe. The power core is intact, but the neural processors look fried." Billy tapped the robot's head. "Something traumatic happened to this fella."

Cristen picked up a small tool from Billy's bench and twirled it between her fingers. "What if it wasn't an accident? What if someone—"

"Deliberately wiped it?" Billy finished her thought. "That's what worries me. Why would someone go through the trouble of erasing a standard service bot?"

"Unless it's not standard at all." Cristen gently set the robot's hand back on the table. "Billy, this could be something big."

Billy flipped the robot's forearm over, his fingers tracing a pattern of scratches that seemed too deliberate to be damage. He grabbed a microfiber cloth, spat on it, and rubbed away years of grime.

"Hey, look at this." He angled the arm toward the light. "There's something engraved here."

Cristen leaned closer, squinting. "Letters? Is that an 'M'?"

Billy's breath caught in his throat. He wiped harder,

revealing three distinct characters etched into the metal: MRA.

"MRA," he whispered, his voice suddenly small in the cluttered room. "Melvin R. Applebaum."

"Your dad?" Cristen's hand flew to her mouth.

Billy nodded, unable to speak. His fingers trembled as they traced the initials. For years, his father had been a ghost, a name rarely spoken in their home. The brilliant engineer who'd vanished when Billy was just one. The man whose absence shaped Billy's life more than his presence ever had.

"This was my dad's." The words felt strange on his tongue. "This robot belonged to my father."

Cristen placed a hand on his shoulder. "Do you think that data unit might—"

"Maybe." Billy's mind raced through possibilities. "If I can extract whatever's stored in there, we might find out what happened to him."

He connected a different set of cables to the data unit, his movements precise despite his shaking hands. The diagnostic screen flickered with encryption warnings.

"It's locked down tight," he muttered. "Military-grade security protocols."

"Can you crack it?"

"I don't know. This is way beyond standard protection." Billy ran a hand through his dark hair. "Whatever's in here, someone really didn't want it found."

Cristen paced behind him, her footsteps light between the scattered parts. "What are you going to do?"

Billy stared at the initials, memories of his father— fragmented and faded—flashing through his mind. The few moments he remembered: large hands guiding his small ones over circuit boards, a deep laugh, the smell of solder and coffee.

"I have to try." He looked up at Cristen, determination hardening his features. "Even if what I find isn't what I want to hear."

Cristen nodded, her green eyes fierce. "Sometimes, you have to fight for answers, even if they scare you."

Billy pocketed the data unit and stashed the robots arm in his backpack. He glanced at Cristen, who gave him an encouraging nod.

"I need to talk to my mom."

They found her in the kitchen, stirring a pot of soup. She looked up with a tired smile that faded when she saw Billy's expression.

"What's wrong, honey?"

Billy placed the robot arm on the counter, the initials facing up. "Mom, I found something at the scrapyard today." He tapped the engraving. "MRA. These are Dad's initials, aren't they?"

His mother's spoon clattered against the pot. She stared at the metal appendage, her face draining of color.

"Where did you find this?" Her voice was barely audible.

"Southern district junkyard." Billy watched her carefully. "Mom, you never talk about Dad. All I know is that he disappeared when I was little."

She wiped her hands on her apron, eyes never leaving the initials. "Melvin Robert Applebaum. Your father always marked his creations." She traced the letters with trembling fingers. "He said a true creator signs their work."

"So this was definitely his?"

She nodded slowly. "Billy, there are things I haven't told you because I thought it would be safer—"

"Safer? What happened to him, Mom?"

She turned off the stove and took a deep breath. "Come with me."

She led Billy and Cristen down the narrow staircase to their basement. In the far corner stood a door Billy had always assumed led to storage—it had been locked for as long as he could remember.

His mother pulled a chain from beneath her shirt, revealing a small key. "Your father's workshop. I sealed it after he disappeared."

The lock clicked open. Dust particles danced in the beam of light as she pushed the door wide.

"I couldn't bear to get rid of his things," she whispered. "But I couldn't face them either."

Billy stepped into the room, his heart pounding. Unlike his chaotic bedroom, his father's workshop was methodically organized. Tools hung on wall-mounted racks. Blueprints were rolled neatly in labeled tubes. Three workbenches stood in a U-formation, each dedicated to different aspects of robotics: mechanics, electronics, and programming.

"It's exactly as he left it," his mother said. "The night before he vanished."

Billy moved through the space, fingers hovering over instruments that hadn't been touched in twelve years. His eyes fell on a framed photo on the desk—his father holding infant Billy, both wearing matching welding goggles pushed up on their foreheads.

"Mom," Billy's voice cracked. "What really happened to him?"

His mother sank into his father's old chair, dust puffing around her. She ran her fingers over the worn armrests, where Melvin's hands had once rested.

"Your father was working on something revolutionary."

Her voice was distant, as if speaking from the past. "A new kind of neural network for combat droids that could learn without becoming dangerous. Ethical programming, he called it."

Billy's eyes swept the workshop, seeing it with new understanding. "Combat droids? Dad built war machines?"

"No," she said sharply. "The opposite. Melvin wanted to change how combat robots functioned. Make them capable of protection without unnecessary violence." She sighed. "But someone else wanted his technology for different purposes."

"Zoltar," Cristen whispered.

Billy's mother looked up, startled. "How did you—"

"Everyone knows about Zoltar's tournaments," Cristen said. "The Combat Arena is infamous."

Billy picked up a blueprint tube labeled "Project Guardian" and carefully extracted the contents. The designs showed a robot similar to the one he'd found in the junkyard.

"Mom, was Dad... taken?" Billy's voice trembled.

She nodded, tears welling. "He knew they were coming. That night, he was frantic, working on something in here. He told me if anything happened, to hide his work until you were old enough to understand." She looked at Billy with sad eyes. "I never thought his past would find its way back to us."

Billy pulled the data unit from his pocket. "I think Dad left a message. This was inside the robot I found."

His mother's eyes widened. "That's his emergency data core. He always carried it." She touched it reverently. "If he managed to hide it in a droid before they took him..."

"Then he wanted someone to find it," Billy finished. He looked around the workshop, seeing not just tools and parts, but his father's legacy. "And now we have."

Cristen squeezed Billy's shoulder. "This could be dangerous."

"I know," Billy said, determination hardening his features. "But this is my father we're talking about. If there's even a chance he's still out there..."

His mother stood, straightening her shoulders. "Melvin always said you had his mind and my heart." She touched Billy's cheek. "He'd be proud of the young man you've become."

Billy clutched the data unit tightly. "I'm going to find out what happened to him. And if he's still alive, I'm bringing him home."

Billy placed the data unit on his father's workbench, connecting it to the old terminal that hadn't been powered on in over a decade. Dust swirled in the beam of the desk lamp as the system hummed to life.

"This encryption is serious," Billy muttered, fingers flying across the keyboard. "Military-grade firewalls, triple authentication protocols."

Cristen leaned over his shoulder. "Can you break through?"

"Maybe, but it'll take time. Dad didn't want just anyone accessing this."

While Billy worked, his mother wandered the workshop, running her fingers over Melvin's tools. She paused at a small charging station in the corner, covered by a tarp.

"I'd forgotten about this," she whispered, pulling the cloth away.

Beneath it sat a small yellow drone, its black underbelly collecting dust. Two mechanical arms hung limp at its sides, and its eyes were dark.

"What is that?" Cristen asked.

"Zippy," Billy's mother answered. "One of Melvin's first companion drones. He was building it for Billy."

As if responding to its name, the drone's systems suddenly whirred to life. Its eyes flickered, then glowed bright blue. The little antennae on top extended with a soft mechanical click.

"Whoa!" Billy spun around. "It's activating!"

Zippy rose unsteadily into the air, wobbling as ancient servos remembered their purpose. It emitted a series of chirps and beeps, hovering in place.

"Is it... scanning us?" Cristen backed away.

The drone turned toward Billy, its optical sensors focusing. It chirped again—a different pattern this time.

"I think it recognizes you," his mother said. "Melvin programmed it with facial recognition."

Zippy zoomed toward the workbench, circling excitedly above the data unit. It extended one of its small mechanical arms, pointing insistently.

"I think it knows what this is," Billy said.

The drone emitted a long, complex series of beeps and whirs. Strangely, Billy found himself understanding the mechanical language.

"It's saying... connection protocol initiated? How do I know that?"

His mother smiled. "Melvin designed Zippy to communicate directly with you. He said you two would speak the same language."

Zippy hovered over the data unit, a small connector extending from its underbelly. Before Billy could stop it, the drone plugged itself into the device.

The terminal screen flickered, encryption barriers falling away. A video file opened automatically.

"It had the decryption key all along," Billy whispered.

The screen filled with his father's face—younger, but unmistakably Melvin Applebaum. Dark circles shadowed his eyes, and his beard was unkept. Behind him, alarms flashed silently.

"Billy," Melvin's recorded voice filled the workshop. "If you're watching this, you've found Zippy and my emergency protocols worked. I don't have much time."

Melvin glanced nervously over his shoulder before continuing.

"Zoltar is coming for me. He wants my neural network designs for his combat droids. What I've created could revolutionize robotics, but in his hands..." Melvin shook his head. "I've hidden the core algorithms throughout my work. Pieces of a puzzle only you can solve."

The recording ended, leaving the workshop in silence. Billy stared at the frozen image of his father's face, searching for familiar features—the same ones he saw in the mirror each morning. The dark hair, the worried brow, the determined set of his jaw. For years, his father had been a phantom, existing only in his mother's careful stories and old photographs.

"I used to dream about him coming home," Billy said quietly, his fingers hovering over the screen. "When I was little, I'd sit by the window on my birthday, thinking maybe today would be the day."

His mother placed a gentle hand on his shoulder. "You stopped asking about him when you turned eight."

"I thought it hurt you too much." Billy swallowed hard. "So I started talking to the machines instead. They didn't cry when I mentioned his name."

Zippy chirped softly, hovering at eye level. The little drone seemed to understand, its mechanical arms gesturing in what looked remarkably like compassion.

Billy turned back to the workbench, spreading out the blueprints from his father's tubes. "These aren't just any designs," he said, voice growing stronger. "These are combat droid schematics. Advanced ones."

Cristen leaned over the papers. "They're incredible. Look at the articulation in these joints—they'd move like water."

"But these power requirements..." Billy pointed to the calculations scribbled in the margins. "These bots would need massive energy sources. Way beyond what we have access to."

He unrolled another blueprint labeled "Guardian Prime." The design showed a humanoid combat droid standing nearly 80 feet tall, with reinforced armor plating and what appeared to be modular weapon systems.

"This one's different," Billy murmured. "Dad wasn't building weapons. He was creating protectors."

His mother nodded. "That's what he always said. The world didn't need more ways to destroy—it needed better ways to defend."

Billy traced the power specifications with his finger. "We'd need industrial-grade fusion cells to even boot this system up. Maybe even military surplus." He looked up, determination hardening his features. "But if we could power it..."

CHAPTER 4: BLUEPRINTS OF COURAGE

Billy didn't sleep that night. Zippy hovered near his desk, occasionally chirping suggestions as Billy scoured the net for information about combat robotics tournaments. His fingers flew across the keyboard, eyes burning from the screen's glow.

"The International Combat Robotics League," he muttered, scrolling through archived footage. "Dad was a champion before he disappeared."

He pulled up tournament brackets from fifteen years ago, tracing his father's path through the competitions. Melvin "The Mechanist" Applebaum had dominated the circuit with designs that were decades ahead of their time.

"Look at this, Zippy." Billy pointed to a match recording. "Dad's bot 'Titan Bolt' took down three opponents simultaneously in the Gauntlet Challenge."

The footage showed a sleek, humanoid robot with reflexes that seemed almost organic, dodging attacks with fluid grace before disabling its opponents with precise strikes.

"These movements... they're exactly like the blueprints we found." Billy leaned closer. "He was testing his designs in plain sight."

Zippy beeped in agreement, projecting a small hologram

of tournament standings. Billy noticed a pattern in the competitors.

"Zoltar Industries sponsored half these teams." He pulled up more recent tournament data. "And after Dad disappeared, they started winning. Every. Single. Year."

By morning, Billy had covered his walls with printouts —tournament brackets, competitor profiles, technical specifications, and news articles about mysterious accidents befalling top engineers. Red string connected related events, forming a web with Zoltar at its center.

Sunlight crept through Billy's window, illuminating the conspiracy board he'd constructed overnight. He rubbed his bloodshot eyes and stretched, joints popping from sitting hunched over for hours.

"Mom's gonna flip when she sees this," he mumbled.

Zippy chirped and bobbed in the air, its antennae twitching as it processed data from Billy's research.

"I know, I know. But look at these power requirements." Billy tapped the blueprints for Titan Bolt. "We'd need an industrial generator just to boot up the systems. Where are we supposed to get that kind of juice?"

He slumped back in his chair, staring at his father's message. Something didn't add up. If Melvin had been captured, why hadn't anyone reported him missing? Why hadn't there been a search?

Billy pulled out his mother's old photo album from under his bed. He flipped through until he found what he was looking for—his parents at the last tournament his father had competed in. In the background stood Zoltar, younger but unmistakable, watching Melvin with an expression that sent chills down Billy's spine.

Billy stuffed the album under his bed as footsteps approached his door. His mother knocked twice before entering, carrying a tray with breakfast.

"You didn't come down—" She froze, taking in the wall of conspiracy theories and scattered blueprints. "Billy, what is all this?"

"Research." He quickly minimized several screens on his computer. Zippy darted behind a pile of spare parts, sensing tension.

His mother set the tray down and picked up one of the tournament brackets. "You've been up all night."

"I'm fine." Billy grabbed a piece of toast and bit into it without enthusiasm.

She sighed, running her fingers over Melvin's photograph. "I've called Aunt Lena. She works in robotics at the university. She can help you understand these blueprints, maybe even—"

"I don't need help." Billy snatched the blueprint from her hands. "I can figure this out myself."

"Billy, your father's work was complex. Even he collaborated with—"

"I said I don't need help!" The words came out sharper than he intended. "This is my project. My responsibility."

His mother's expression hardened. "This isn't just about robots anymore, is it? You think your father's alive."

Billy turned away, focusing on a circuit diagram. "Dad's message was clear. Someone took him. And no one even looked for him."

"We did look. For months." Her voice cracked. "The police, private investigators—"

"Well, they didn't look hard enough." Billy gestured at his research. "Zoltar's tournaments, the missing engineers, Dad's blueprints—it's all connected."

She reached for his shoulder. "Let me call Lena. She has resources, connections—"

"No." Billy stepped back. "The fewer people who know, the safer we'll be. Dad trusted me with this message, not Aunt Lena."

"You're thirteen, Billy."

"I'm also the only one who can read Dad's code." He tapped his head. "And I have Zippy. We don't need anyone else slowing us down."

His mother stared at him for a long moment. "You're just like him. Stubborn to a fault."

"Good." Billy turned back to his workbench. "Then you know I'll find him."

Billy spread the tournament flyer across his desk, Zippy hovering anxiously overhead. The bold red letters seemed to mock him: "ZOLTAR'S 15TH ANNUAL COMBAT ROBOTICS CHAMPIONSHIP - 5 WEEKS FROM TODAY."

"Five weeks." He collapsed into his chair, running calculations in his head. "That's barely enough time to understand Dad's blueprints, let alone build anything combat-ready."

Zippy chirped a series of concerned beeps, its eyes dimming slightly.

"I know it's impossible." Billy grabbed a screwdriver and twirled it between his fingers. "But it's also our only shot at getting inside Zoltar Industries."

He pulled up the tournament requirements on his tablet. Entry fees, weight classes, safety protocols—and the kicker: all participants under 16 required adult supervision.

"Great." Billy tossed the tablet onto his bed. "Even if I could build something, they wouldn't let me compete without a guardian."

His eyes drifted to the basement door. His father's workshop contained everything he needed—tools, parts, expertise captured in notes and diagrams. But translating those resources into a functioning combat robot in five weeks? When professional teams took months?

Zippy nudged a blueprint toward him, beeping insistently.

"Yeah, I see it." Billy picked up the sheet, studying the modular design of Titan Bolt's smaller prototype. "We don't need to build the whole thing. Just enough to qualify."

He grabbed a marker and circled components on the blueprint—core power system, basic mobility, simplified combat arms. The bare minimum needed for a functioning entry.

"If we work around the clock..." He trailed off, already mentally cataloging the parts they'd need to scavenge. "And if I can figure out that power problem..."

Zippy projected a small calendar, marking off the days until the tournament.

"Thirty-five days." Billy pinned the tournament flyer to his wall, right in the center of his research web. "Dad spent years perfecting these designs. I've got five weeks."

He grabbed his tool belt and slipped his welding goggles onto his head.

"Let's get to work."

The basement workshop felt different at night. Billy's flashlight cast long shadows across his father's equipment as he descended the stairs, Zippy floating ahead like a luminous scout. The air smelled of metal and dust, untouched potential waiting to be awakened.

"Dad's power coupling diagrams should be in that cabinet," Billy whispered, though there was no need for secrecy. His mother had finally fallen asleep after hovering anxiously all day.

He pulled open the heavy metal drawer, rifling through meticulously labeled folders until he found what he needed. The schematics were complex—far beyond standard robotics—with notations in his father's distinctive handwriting.

"Look at this, Zippy." Billy spread the diagrams across the workbench. "Dad developed a miniaturized fusion cell. That's how Titan Bolt maintained such high output without overheating."

Zippy chirped skeptically, its sensors scanning the designs.

"I know it sounds impossible." Billy traced the intricate power routing system with his finger. "But these calculations check out. The problem is getting enough initial charge to kickstart the reaction."

He rummaged through storage bins, pulling out components his father had collected—specialized alloys, custom circuit boards, experimental power cells. Some parts were dusty but intact; others would need significant restoration.

"We need to start small." Billy cleared a space on the workbench and pulled up a stool. "If we can get a prototype fusion cell working at quarter capacity, we can scale up from there."

For hours, Billy worked under the single workshop light, carefully assembling a miniature version of his father's power system. His hands moved with surprising confidence, as if the knowledge was somehow encoded in his DNA. Occasionally, he'd pause to consult the blueprints or ask Zippy to scan a component.

Near dawn, he connected the final wire to his cobbled-together power cell. It was ugly—nothing like his father's elegant designs—but the principles were sound.

"Diagnostic check," Billy muttered, attaching monitoring equipment. "If this works, we'll have enough power to begin testing the mobility systems."

Zippy retreated to a safe distance, beeping nervously.

"Yeah, stand back." Billy adjusted his welding goggles and took a deep breath. "Three... two... one..."

He flipped the switch.

The makeshift fusion cell hummed to life, its core glowing with an eerie blue light. Readings spiked on Billy's monitors, power levels climbing steadily until—

A sharp crack echoed through the basement as the cell overloaded. Sparks showered across the workbench. Billy ducked, shielding his face as the cell's containment field collapsed.

"No, no, no!" He lunged for the emergency cutoff switch, killing power to the entire workshop. Darkness engulfed them, broken only by Zippy's concerned glow and the dying embers of fried circuitry.

Billy slumped against the workbench, pushing his goggles up to rub his eyes. "Dad made it look so easy."

Zippy hovered closer, projecting the failed component schematics with suggested modifications.

"The containment field couldn't handle the load." Billy picked through the smoking remains of his prototype. "We need better insulation for the core. And the power regulation system is too basic."

He checked his watch—5:47 AM. He'd been working for nearly eight hours straight.

"Mom'll be up soon." He began gathering his tools. "We'll have to continue tonight."

Zippy chirped questioningly, gesturing toward a locked cabinet in the corner of the workshop.

"Dad's restricted projects?" Billy frowned. "Mom said that

cabinet was off-limits."

Zippy projected an image from the blueprints they'd found—a specialized containment system that matched the cabinet's dimensions.

Billy hesitated, then pulled out a small pick set from his tool belt. "If Dad's advanced prototypes are in there, they could save us weeks of work."

The lock clicked open after a minute of careful manipulation. Inside, Billy found exactly what they needed—a palm-sized fusion cell, perfectly preserved in a protective case.

"This is it." Billy lifted the device reverently. Unlike his crude attempt, this was a marvel of engineering —elegant, compact, and based on the diagnostic panel, fully functional. "Dad already solved the containment problem."

Zippy beeped excitedly, scanning the cell's specifications.

"With this as our power core..." Billy's mind raced with possibilities. "We might actually have a chance."

Billy hunched over his workbench, fingers flying across a tablet as he finalized Titan Bolt's registration details. Three days until the deadline, and he still hadn't solved his biggest problem.

"Adult supervision required," he muttered, rubbing his temples. "How am I supposed to fake that?"

Zippy hovered nearby, projecting holographic tournament regulations that Billy had already memorized. The drone chirped a suggestion, displaying an ID forgery program.

"No way." Billy shook his head. "Security at Zoltar's events uses biometric scanning. We'd never get past the entrance."

He'd spent two weeks rebuilding the miniature version

of Titan Bolt. The combat robot now stood three feet tall in the corner of his room—a masterpiece of engineering that incorporated his father's fusion cell. Its sleek black chassis gleamed under the workshop lights, compact arms folded across its chest. The programming was nearly complete, combat routines loaded and ready for testing.

All that work, and he might not even get through the door.

"Maybe I could ask Mr. Henson?" Billy considered the retired mechanic who lived down the street. "He knows robots."

Zippy beeped disapprovingly, displaying newspaper clippings about Zoltar's security forces.

"You're right. Can't risk putting anyone else in danger." Billy slumped in his chair. "Mom would never agree to it, and anyone who helps me could become a target."

He scrolled through the tournament brackets from previous years, studying the registration patterns. Most entries came from corporate teams or university research programs. Individual competitors were rare—and successful ones even rarer.

"Wait." Billy zoomed in on a detail he'd missed before. "Look at this exception clause."

The fine print stated that previous champions or their direct descendants could petition for special registration status, including modified supervision requirements for legacy competitors.

"Dad was a five-time champion." Billy's heart raced as he pulled up the petition form. "I qualify as a legacy competitor."

Zippy chirped uncertainly, highlighting the verification process.

"They'll check my DNA against their records." Billy grinned. "And guess what? Dad's genetic profile is already in their system from his competing days."

He began filling out the form, hope building with each field completed. This could work. This had to work.

The legacy competitor application came through three days later. Billy clutched the confirmation in his trembling hands, the holographic Zoltar Industries logo shimmering above his tablet.

"We're in, Zippy." His voice barely rose above a whisper. "We're actually in."

Zippy circled excitedly, beeping a victory tune that echoed through Billy's room. The miniature Titan Bolt stood in the corner, its systems humming with quiet power, ready for its first real test.

Billy moved to his window, staring out at the sprawling cityscape of Biome Synthesis. Somewhere out there, beyond the towering buildings and artificial forests, was Zoltar Industries—and his father.

"Twelve years." Billy's breath fogged the glass. "Twelve tournaments since Dad disappeared. And Zoltar's been winning every single one."

He turned back to his room, to the wall of evidence he'd compiled. Photos of missing engineers. Tournament brackets. News clippings about technological breakthroughs from Zoltar Industries that seemed to appear right after prominent roboticists vanished.

"It stops now." Billy clenched his fists. "Dad didn't just leave us. He was taken because he was too good, because he knew too much."

Zippy hovered closer, projecting a small hologram of Melvin from an old tournament video. The resemblance between father and son was striking—the same determined set of the jaw, the same intensity in their eyes.

"I'm going to win this tournament." Billy touched the hologram, his fingers passing through his father's face. "And when I do, I'm going to find him. I don't care what security systems Zoltar has, what guards or robots or whatever else he's hiding behind."

He walked to Titan Bolt, placing his hand on the robot's cool metal shoulder.

"Dad built you to protect people. Now we're going to use you to save him."

Zippy chirped a warning, displaying tournament statistics showing the brutal elimination rounds.

"I know it's dangerous." Billy's voice hardened. "But Zoltar doesn't know what's coming. He thinks he's just getting another competitor. What he's really getting is me."

CHAPTER 5: WHISPERS OF THE FALLEN

The Iron Graveyard loomed before Billy, a jagged skyline of broken robots and discarded parts stretching toward the horizon. Dawn light filtered through smog, casting everything in a sickly orange glow. He adjusted his welding goggles over his eyes, protecting them from the acidic dust that swirled through the scrapyard.

"Just what we need, Zippy." Billy consulted the holographic schematic the drone projected. "Three class-seven hydraulic actuators, fusion cell connectors, and a primary control matrix."

Zippy beeped skeptically, highlighting the danger zones on the map.

"I know, I know. The outer ring is safer, but those parts are picked clean.' Billy trudged deeper into the graveyard, boots crunching on fragments of metal. "What we need is in the heart of this place."

He climbed over the shell of an ancient war machine, its cannon now nothing but a rusted tube. The further in he went, the larger and more intact the discarded robots became. Many bore scorch marks or impact damage— casualties of tournaments past.

"Look at that." Billy pointed to a half-buried titan-class robot. "Those shoulder joints might work for Titan's primary locomotion system."

He approached the fallen giant, its metal skin peeling away in layers. Carefully, he pried open an access panel and began disconnecting the actuator he needed.

"Almost got it..." His fingers worked nimbly, disconnecting power lines and control circuits.

The ground trembled. Billy froze.

"Zippy, what was—"

A violent shudder rippled through the scrapyard. The titan's eyes flickered red, its systems powering up despite decades of dormancy.

"Power surge!" Billy scrambled backward as the massive robot's remaining arm swung wildly, its programming corrupted by years of decay. "The whole grid is activating!"

All around him, dead machines twitched and groaned. Maintenance bots skittered on broken legs. A security drone rose unsteadily into the air, weapons systems trying to target anything that moved.

Billy ducked behind a pile of scrapped chassis as energy discharges crackled through the air. The titan lurched forward, dragging itself with its one functioning arm, systems caught in a destructive loop.

"We need to get out of here!" Billy called to Zippy, who darted between energy blasts, recording everything. "That main power conduit must have overloaded!"

Billy dove behind the crumbling remains of a security droid as a volley of energy blasts scorched the ground where he'd stood seconds before. His heart hammered against his ribs.

"Zippy! Distraction protocol!"

The little drone chirped affirmatively and shot upward, releasing a burst of electromagnetic pulses that confused the reanimated machines' targeting systems. Billy seized his chance, sprinting toward a narrow corridor between towering piles of scrap.

A massive hydraulic arm crashed down inches from his head. He stumbled, nearly losing his footing on the treacherous ground. The titan dragged itself closer, its corrupted systems fixated on eliminating the intruder.

"This was stupid," Billy gasped, squeezing through a gap between two derelict transports. "So stupid!"

A security drone spotted him, its damaged weapons system firing wildly. Shrapnel sliced across Billy's forearm, drawing blood. He hissed in pain but kept moving.

"Dad wouldn't have made these rookie mistakes," he muttered, ducking under a low-hanging mess of cables. "He'd have brought proper equipment, done recon..."

The ground gave way beneath him. Billy plummeted several feet before catching himself on a jutting piece of metal. Below him, a pit of jagged components waited to impale anyone unlucky enough to fall.

Zippy swooped down, extending its small mechanical arms to help pull him up.

"Thanks, buddy." Billy hauled himself to safety, breathing hard. "We're out of our depth here."

He glanced back at the chaos of reactivated machines. The parts he needed remained tantalizingly out of reach, but the risk had become too great.

"If I die out here, no one will ever know what happened to Dad." The thought struck him like a physical blow. "Mom would be alone. Just like he left us alone."

Billy imagined his room gathering dust, his projects abandoned. His mother growing old, with two ghosts haunting her instead of one. No answers, no closure—just emptiness stretching into the years ahead.

Zippy nudged his shoulder, beeping urgently. The titan had spotted them again.

"You're right. Time to go."

Billy and Zippy navigated through the maze of scrap, the titan's thunderous movements growing distant behind them. They reached the perimeter of the Iron Graveyard, Billy's lungs burning with each breath. He leaned against a stack of crushed service droids, wiping sweat from his forehead.

"That was close." He examined the cut on his arm. "Too close."

Zippy chirped in agreement, hovering protectively nearby.

"Well, well. If it isn't the orphan and his flying trash can."

Billy's head snapped up. Relson emerged from behind a pile of discarded parts, flanked by two other teenagers. The bully wore his signature leather jacket, a size too large, the sleeves rolled up to hide the fact.

"I'm not an orphan," Billy muttered, straightening up despite his exhaustion. "And Zippy's not trash."

Relson circled Billy, eyes gleaming with malice. "What are you doing in the deep zones, Applebaum? This isn't a playground for babies."

"None of your business." Billy tried to step around him, but Relson blocked his path.

"Everything in this sector is my business." Relson's gaze fell to the tool belt around Billy's waist. "What'd you find in there? Anything good?"

"Nothing. The surge activated the old bots. It's a death trap in there now."

Relson laughed, but his eyes darted nervously toward the interior of the graveyard. "You expect me to believe that? You're just trying to keep the good salvage for yourself."

"Believe what you want." Billy's fingers tightened around a small EMP device in his pocket—a last resort. "I need to get home."

"Not until you pay the toll." Relson held out his hand. "Tools or parts. Your choice."

Zippy buzzed angrily, positioning itself between Billy and the bully.

"Your little drone won't save you." Relson stepped closer. "I heard you've been asking about the tournament. What's the matter? Daddy issues got you thinking you're fighter material now?"

Billy's face flushed hot. "At least my father was somebody. Who was yours again? Oh right, nobody knows."

Relson's smirk vanished. He lunged forward, grabbing Billy by the collar of his engineer's jacket. "Say that again, gear-head. I dare you."

Relson's knuckles whitened as he tightened his grip on Billy's jacket. The two boys locked eyes, neither willing to back down.

"Truth hurts, doesn't it?" Billy said, his voice steadier than he felt.

Zippy darted nervously around them, emitting high-pitched warning beeps. The drone's sensors detected something the humans hadn't noticed yet—the ground trembling beneath their feet.

"You think you're better than everyone because your dad was some hotshot engineer?" Relson shoved Billy against a pile of scrap. "News flash, Bolts—he abandoned you. Left you behind like broken parts."

The words stung worse than the cut on Billy's arm. He swallowed hard, refusing to show how deeply they cut.

"At least I know who he was," Billy countered. "At least I have something to—"

A deafening crash interrupted him as a security drone burst through a wall of scrap twenty yards away, its targeting systems sweeping the area. All four boys froze.

"You weren't kidding," Relson whispered, his anger momentarily forgotten.

The drone pivoted, its damaged sensors locking onto the group. A weapon port on its underside began to glow ominously.

"Run!" Billy yelled, shoving Relson aside as an energy blast scorched the ground where they'd been standing.

Relson's two friends scattered, disappearing into the maze of metal. The drone advanced, its hover jets kicking up clouds of metallic dust.

Billy pulled the EMP device from his pocket. "I've only got one shot with this."

Relson's eyes widened. "You'll fry every piece of tech in a thirty-foot radius!"

"Better than being fried ourselves." Billy twisted the device's activation dial. "On my mark, dive behind that crusher unit."

Surprisingly, Relson nodded, tensing for the sprint.

"Now!"

They bolted in opposite directions as the drone fired again. Billy slid behind cover, counted to three, and hurled the EMP device. It arced through the air, landing directly beneath the drone.

A pulse of blue energy erupted outward. The drone seized up mid-air, then crashed to the ground in a shower of sparks. Zippy, having wisely retreated to a safe distance, zoomed back to Billy's side.

Relson emerged from his hiding spot, staring at the disabled drone with newfound respect.

"You made that?" he asked, nodding toward the spent

EMP device.

Billy dusted himself off, examining the fallen drone. "Yeah, I made it. Repurposed parts from an old communication jammer."

Relson kicked at the disabled machine, whistling low. "That's... actually impressive."

"Thanks." Billy knelt to retrieve what remained of his device. Their eyes met, the tension between them shifting into something uncertain.

Relson cleared his throat. "Look, about what I said—"

"Forget it." Billy waved him off, surprising himself with the gesture. "We've all got our stuff."

"Yeah." Relson shuffled his feet, then extended his hand. "Truce? At least until we're out of this death trap?"

Billy hesitated, then shook it. "Truce."

They navigated the outer rim of the scrapyard in tense silence, Zippy scouting ahead for dangers. When they reached the boundary fence, Relson paused.

"So what were you really doing in there? Nobody risks the deep zone without a reason."

Billy considered lying, then decided against it. "I'm entering the tournament."

Relson's eyebrows shot up. "You? In the Combat Arena?"

"Yeah, me." Billy's jaw tightened. "I've got my reasons."

"You'd need a serious machine for that. And a power source that could—" Relson stopped, understanding dawning. "That's what you were looking for in there."

Billy nodded. "I've got the prototype robot. My dad built it. But I need a larger chassis to build the combat version and a class-nine fusion cell to power the upgrades I've designed."

Relson's expression shifted from skepticism to intrigue. "Class-nine fusion cells are rare. The only ones I've seen are in the military sector."

"I know." Billy sighed, frustration evident in his slumped shoulders. "Without it, I can't power the advanced hydraulics or the defensive systems."

Zippy chirped and projected a holographic image— schematics for a modified power distribution system.

"Even if you had the cell, you'd need a buffer array to regulate the output." Relson studied the projection with unexpected technical understanding. "Otherwise, you'd fry your circuits the moment you powered up."

Billy stared at him, surprised. "You know about power systems?"

Relson shrugged, suddenly self-conscious. "My uncle works maintenance at the old power plant. I help out sometimes."

"Huh." Billy considered this new information. "I figured you just broke things, not fixed them."

"There's a lot you don't know about me, Applebaum." Relson kicked at the ground. "Why are you so set on the tournament anyway? The odds of a first-timer surviving the qualifiers are basically zero."

Billy hesitated, weighing how much to reveal. "It's about my dad. I think... I think he's still alive. And Zoltar has him."

Relson's eyes widened. "Zoltar? The tournament master? That's—"

"Crazy, I know." Billy's voice hardened. "But I found a message. And blueprints. It all points to the tournament."

An uncomfortable silence stretched between them. Finally, Relson spoke.

"I might know someone who can help with the fusion cell."

"Seriously?" Billy couldn't hide his surprise.

"Don't get excited. It's dangerous, and they don't do charity." Relson hesitated.

"Why would you help me?"

Relson's face darkened. "Let's just say I understand what it's like to have questions about family that nobody wants to answer."

Before Billy could respond, Zippy emitted an urgent series of beeps. The drone's sensors had detected movement at the perimeter fence—security patrols.

"We need to move," Relson hissed, pulling Billy behind a massive scrap compactor. "Security drones sweep this sector every hour."

They crouched in silence as the patrol passed overhead, searchlights cutting through the dusty air. When the coast was clear, Relson continued in a hushed voice.

"There's someone who might help you. Goes by 'The Caveman.' Used to be a champion in the arena—one of the best robot engineers ever. Story goes he won Zoltar's tournament years ago, then disappeared."

Billy's eyes widened. "Disappeared how?"

"Nobody knows for sure." Relson glanced nervously at the sky. "Some say Zoltar tried to imprison him like the others, but he escaped. Built himself a hideout somewhere under the scrapyard, deep in the tunnel systems."

"Under the scrapyard?" Billy repeated, skepticism evident in his voice. "Nobody could survive down there. The radiation levels alone would—"

"He found a way." Relson cut him off. "My uncle's seen him—or thinks he has. Says the guy's gone full primitive. Sworn off technology after what Zoltar did to him."

Zippy chirped questioningly, hovering closer.

"I know, it sounds crazy," Relson admitted. "But people

who venture deep enough into the scrapyard sometimes find things—tools, parts—fixed and left out, like someone's watching over the place."

Billy frowned. "If he's sworn off technology, why would he help me build a combat robot?"

"I didn't say it would be easy." Relson shrugged. "But if anyone knows how to beat Zoltar at his own game, it's the Caveman. Real name's Juno Kett, if the stories are true."

"Juno Kett..." Billy repeated, the name triggering something in his memory. "I think my dad mentioned him in his journals. They worked together, before..."

"Before Zoltar got your dad?" Relson finished.

Billy nodded slowly. "How do I find him?"

"That's the hard part. The tunnels under the scrapyard are a maze, and the deeper sections are crawling with rogue security systems and half-functioning killer bots." Relson hesitated. "But there's an entrance near the old water reclamation plant. It's the safest way in—relatively speaking."

Billy stared at Relson, processing this unexpected turn. The Caveman—a tournament champion who escaped Zoltar and now lived beneath the scrapyard. It sounded impossible, yet somehow it fit perfectly into the bizarre puzzle his life had become.

"I need to find him," Billy decided. "If he worked with my dad and escaped from Zoltar, he might know where they're keeping him."

Relson nodded, then glanced at the darkening sky. "The tunnels are a labyrinth—you could wander for weeks down there."

"I don't have weeks." Billy's jaw set with determination. "I'll have to be smarter, not just lucky."

Zippy beeped excitedly, projecting a holographic map of

the district. The drone highlighted the water reclamation plant and calculated potential routes.

"Your little bot's pretty impressive," Relson admitted grudgingly.

"He's not just a bot. He's my friend." Billy patted Zippy affectionately. "And he's good at finding patterns where others see chaos."

They reached the edge of the scrapyard as twilight deepened the shadows around them. The city's lights blinked on in the distance, a constellation of artificial stars against the polluted sky.

"I should head back," Relson said, suddenly awkward again. "My crew will wonder where I disappeared to."

Billy nodded. "Thanks. For the information about the Caveman."

"Don't thank me yet. You might not like what you find down there." Relson hesitated. "And Applebaum? If you do make it to the tournament... try not to die, okay? Would be a waste of talent."

With that backhanded compliment, Relson slipped away into the gathering darkness, leaving Billy and Zippy alone at the edge of the Iron Graveyard.

"Come on, Zippy," Billy murmured. "We need to plan an expedition."

The drone chirped in agreement, hovering close to Billy's shoulder as they turned toward home, the weight of their new mission settling around them like the evening gloom.

CHAPTER 6: GEARS OF DEFIANCE

Cristen arrived at Billy's house the next morning, her tech bow slung over her shoulder. She hadn't heard from him in two days, which was unusual. Billy might be obsessive about his projects, but he always responded to her messages eventually.

She raised her hand to knock when a figure approached from the opposite direction. Her muscles tensed instinctively.

Relson stopped short when he spotted her. "What are you doing here?"

"I could ask you the same thing." Cristen's eyes narrowed. "Since when do you visit Billy?"

"Since it's none of your business." Relson crossed his arms defensively.

Cristen sized him up. "If you're here to mess with him—"

"I'm not." Relson glanced at the house, then back at her. "I'm helping him with something."

"You? Helping?" She couldn't keep the disbelief from her voice. "Last I checked, you were shoving him into lockers."

"Things change." Relson kicked at the ground. "Found him in the scrapyard yesterday. We talked."

Cristen studied his face, searching for deception. "About what?"

"The tournament. His dad." Relson hesitated. "The

Caveman."

"The what?"

"Not what—who. Some old champion living under the scrapyard." Relson shrugged. "Billy thinks this guy might help him build a bot for the tournament."

Cristen's eyes widened. "And you believe this... caveman exists?"

"My uncle's seen him." Relson's defensiveness returned. "Why are you here, anyway?"

"Billy's been off-grid for days. I was worried." She fidgeted with her bow strap. "The tournament's dangerous. He can't just rush in without a plan."

An awkward silence fell between them—two people with nothing in common except concern for the same stubborn boy.

"Well," Relson finally said, "are we gonna knock or what?"

Cristen nodded, reaching for the door just as a crash sounded from inside, followed by Billy's muffled cursing.

Billy yanked the door open, his welding goggles askew and face smudged with grease. He froze at the sight of both Cristen and Relson standing there together.

"Are you two... talking to each other?" He blinked rapidly. "Did I cross into another dimension?"

"We were just discussing your disappearing act," Cristen pushed past him into the cluttered living room. "And this cave expedition Relson mentioned."

Billy shot Relson an accusatory look. "Thanks for the heads-up."

"What? She was already here." Relson followed them inside, carefully navigating around piles of mechanical parts.

Cristen spun to face Billy. "You can't seriously be planning to go into some cave system beneath the scrapyard based on a rumor."

"It's not just a rumor." Billy pulled a crumpled map from his pocket, spreading it across his workbench. "I've been piecing this together from Dad's notes. See these markings? They match exactly where Relson says people have spotted The Caveman."

"Even if he exists," Cristen argued, "what makes you think he'll help you?"

"He was a champion, like my dad." Billy's voice softened. "And he escaped from Zoltar. He might know something —anything—about what happened."

"Or he could be completely insane after living underground for years," Cristen countered. "Billy, those caves could collapse. There could be toxic gases, abandoned security systems—"

"I've thought of all that." Billy pointed to a small collection of gear in the corner—ropes, makeshift gas masks, flashlights. "I'm not going in blind."

"We're not going in blind," Relson corrected, earning surprised looks from both of them. "What? I know the way in. My uncle showed me once."

Cristen threw up her hands. "This is insane. Both of you."

Billy placed a hand on her shoulder. "I need to do this, Cris. My dad's been gone my whole life. If there's even a chance..."

"Fine," she sighed, studying the map. "But I'm coming too. Someone needs to keep you idiots alive."

"So we're doing this?" Relson asked.

The afternoon sun beat down on the scrapyard, turning the metal landscape into a shimmering mirage of heat and rust. Relson led the way, weaving through towering piles of discarded robots with surprising confidence. Billy followed close behind, his tool belt jingling with each step, while Cristen brought up the rear, her bow ready as she scanned for any signs of danger.

"How much further?" Billy wiped sweat from his brow, adjusting his welding goggles.

"Almost there." Relson paused at a junction between two massive heaps of scrap. "My uncle only showed me once, but I remember it was past the big lifter unit."

Cristen frowned. "There are dozens of lifter units here."

"Not like this one." Relson pointed ahead to an enormous industrial loader, its chassis partially collapsed and fused with the ground. "That thing was used to build the outer wall before the synthetics took over construction."

They approached the fallen giant cautiously. Its shadow provided momentary relief from the heat, but the air beneath it felt stagnant, heavy with the scent of oxidized metal.

"Here." Relson knelt beside what appeared to be just another pile of twisted wires and plating. He pushed aside a panel, revealing a dark opening. "Uncle said he followed The Caveman to this spot, but was too scared to go further."

Billy crouched beside him, peering into the darkness. "This could just be a drainage system."

"Look." Relson pointed to faint markings etched into the metal around the opening—similar to the symbols on Billy's map. "These weren't made by any machine."

Cristen leaned in, her expression softening with surprise. "They match your father's notes."

Billy pulled out a small light from his belt, illuminating a makeshift ladder descending into darkness. The rungs were welded from robot limbs, their joints repurposed into sturdy handholds.

"Someone built this," he whispered, excitement

overtaking caution. "Someone who knows how to repurpose tech."

Relson nodded. "The Caveman."

"Or it could be maintenance workers," Cristen countered, though her skepticism sounded weaker now. "Or scavengers."

"Only one way to find out." Billy secured his goggles and switched on his headlamp. "I'll go first."

Relson grabbed his arm. "No way. I found it, I go first."

"This isn't about—"

"Both of you, stop." Cristen pulled out three small devices from her pocket. "Sync these first. They're short-range communicators. If we get separated down there, at least we can find each other."

They attached the devices to their wrists, the small screens glowing with three blinking dots.

"Ready?" Relson asked, already lowering himself onto the ladder.

The ladder creaked under their weight as they descended into darkness. Billy counted the rungs—twenty-seven—before his feet touched solid ground. The air grew cooler, a welcome relief from the scorching heat above, but carried an unsettling stillness that made the hairs on his neck stand up.

"Everyone okay?" he whispered, his voice echoing slightly in the narrow passage.

"Define okay," Cristen muttered, stepping off the ladder. Her headlamp cut through the darkness, revealing rough stone walls reinforced with salvaged metal struts. "This place feels... alive somehow."

Relson snorted. "It's a cave, not a monster."

"I didn't mean—" She stopped suddenly. "Look."

Their lights illuminated patches of pale blue-green

moss growing along the damp stone, emitting a faint bioluminescent glow.

"That's not natural," Billy murmured, leaning closer. "This species shouldn't grow underground without UV light."

"Maybe it's engineered," Relson suggested. "Like the stuff they use in the hydroponics sector."

Billy nodded, impressed by Relson's observation. "Good thinking. Someone's been cultivating this."

They followed the narrow passage as it wound deeper beneath the scrapyard. Occasionally, their lights would catch glimpses of technology embedded in the stone—old circuit boards, repurposed wiring, sensors disguised as rocks.

"Someone's monitoring this tunnel," Billy whispered, pointing to a camera lens camouflaged as a mineral deposit.

"Great," Cristen sighed. "So much for the element of surprise."

The passage suddenly widened, opening into a vast chamber that stole their breath. Above them, shafts of filtered sunlight pierced through what appeared to be the underside of the scrapyard. The effect was mesmerizing —golden light streaming through gaps in the robot parts overhead, casting strange, shifting patterns on the stone floor.

"It's beautiful," Cristen whispered.

Billy stared upward, understanding dawning on his face. "Those aren't random gaps. Someone engineered those skylights." He pointed to translucent alloy plates strategically placed among the junk. "They're refracting and amplifying the sunlight."

"Guys," Relson's voice was unusually tense. He pointed to the far side of the chamber where a small fire burned in a stone pit. Beside it sat a hunched figure, motionless in the dancing shadows.

The figure spoke without turning. "Three children, stumbling into my home." His voice was rough from disuse. "Either very brave or very foolish."

The figure rose in one fluid motion, unnaturally fast for someone who appeared so hunched and frail moments before. Before they could react, he lunged toward them with a primal roar, his wild hair and beard creating a terrifying silhouette against the firelight.

"INTRUDERS!" The Caveman bellowed, brandishing what looked like a spear fashioned from robot parts. His eyes were wide and feral, his face contorted into a mask of rage.

Cristen stumbled backward, nearly dropping her bow as she raised her arms defensively. Billy froze in place, his mouth hanging open in shock.

"We're not—" Billy started to explain, but his words were cut short as the Caveman charged forward again, swinging the makeshift weapon in a wide arc that whistled through the air inches from their faces.

"LEAVE! LEAVE NOW!" The man's voice echoed throughout the chamber, amplified by the natural acoustics of the cave. His appearance was even more startling up close—clothes made from scavenged materials, skin weathered and marked with strange symbols similar to those on Billy's map.

Relson's composure shattered. The tough exterior he'd maintained crumbled as primal fear took over. Without a word, he spun around and bolted back toward the tunnel entrance, his footsteps echoing frantically against the stone floor.

"Relson, wait!" Billy called after him, but the boy was

already disappearing into the darkness of the passage.

The Caveman let out a disturbing laugh that bounced off the walls. "One down," he growled, turning his attention back to Billy and Cristen. "Two to go."

Cristen's fingers tightened around her bow, but she didn't run. Instead, she stepped slightly in front of Billy, her stance protective despite the tremor in her hands.

"We just want to talk," she said, her voice steadier than she felt. "About Melvin Applebaum."

The Caveman froze at the mention of Melvin's name, his wild eyes narrowing with suspicion. The makeshift spear lowered slightly, though his knuckles remained white around its shaft.

"Applebaum?" The word came out as a harsh whisper. "How do you know that name?"

Billy slowly raised his hands, palms forward. "He's my father."

The Caveman circled them like a predator, studying Billy's face with unnerving intensity. His gaze lingered on Billy's welding goggles perched atop his head, then dropped to the tool belt around his waist.

"Prove it," he demanded, jabbing the spear toward Billy. "Anyone could claim to be Melvin's son."

Billy swallowed hard. His hand trembled slightly as he reached into his pocket and pulled out a small object—a brass gear with intricate engravings around its edge. "He made this. It's from his first combat robot."

The Caveman snatched it from Billy's palm with surprising speed. He turned it over in his dirt-encrusted fingers, then held it up to one of the shafts of light streaming down from above. After a long moment, his shoulders sagged, and the feral energy that had animated him moments before seemed to drain away.

"Sit," he muttered, gesturing toward the small fire. "But keep your distance."

Billy and Cristen exchanged glances before cautiously approaching the fire pit. They sat cross-legged on the smooth stone floor while the Caveman retreated to a makeshift chair constructed from robot parts.

"My name is Juno Kett," the man said, his voice steadier now. "Your father called me 'The Caveman' as a joke. It stuck." He stared into the flames. "Why are you here?"

Billy took a deep breath. "My father disappeared when I was a baby. All my life, I thought he abandoned us." He glanced at Cristen, who nodded encouragingly. "But three days ago, I found a message he left behind. He didn't leave —he was taken by Zoltar after winning the tournament."

Juno's head snapped up, his eyes suddenly alert. "And now you want to enter the tournament yourself." It wasn't a question.

"Yes," Billy admitted. "It's the only way I can get close to Zoltar, find out what happened to my dad."

"Suicide," Juno spat. "You're just a child."

"I'm his son," Billy countered, his voice growing stronger. "I've been studying his blueprints, his combat strategies. I can build a robot that can win, but I need a power source strong enough to make it work."

CHAPTER 7: SHADOWS OF VALOR

Juno's face darkened as he tossed another piece of scrap into the fire. The flames cast jagged shadows across his weathered face, highlighting the scars that told stories of battles long past.

"No." The word fell heavy between them. "I won't help you."

"But—" Billy started.

"I said no!" Juno slammed his fist against the metal arm of his makeshift chair. "You have no idea what you're asking. No idea what Zoltar is capable of."

Cristen leaned forward. "That's exactly why Billy needs your help. He's going to do this with or without—"

"Then he'll die with or without me," Juno cut her off. His eyes locked with Billy's. "Your father was brilliant. The best engineer I'd ever seen. And even he couldn't escape Zoltar's clutches. What chance do you think you have?"

Billy's jaw tightened. "My father left me a message. He believed I could help him."

"Your father was desperate," Juno said, his voice dropping to a harsh whisper. "I escaped. Barely. Lived in these caves for years, watching the world above through cracks in the junkyard. Watching Zoltar's empire grow while good people disappeared into his laboratories."

He stood suddenly, pacing the perimeter of the fire.

"I swore I'd never touch technology again. Never build another machine for that monster to corrupt."

"My father isn't dead," Billy insisted. "I can feel it."

"Maybe not." Juno stopped pacing, his silhouette stark against the cave wall. "But I'm dead to that world up there. And I plan to stay that way."

Cristen's brow furrowed. "So you'll just hide down here forever? While Zoltar takes more people like Melvin?"

"Yes." Juno's face was stone. "I fought my battle. I lost everything that mattered. My freedom. My sanity." He gestured around the cave. "This is all I have left."

"But you won the tournament," Billy said. "You know how to beat Zoltar's champions."

"And what did winning get me?" Juno laughed bitterly. "A prison cell in Zoltar's compound. Three years of my life building weapons I never wanted to create." He shook his head. "No. Find another way, boy. I'm done with Zoltar's games."

Billy stood, his fists clenched at his sides. The firelight caught the metal accents on his denim jacket, sending reflections dancing across the cave walls.

"I understand being afraid," he said, voice steady despite the tension. "But my father's out there. He's been locked away for years while I grew up thinking he abandoned us. And now I find out he's been trapped by some tech-obsessed madman?"

Billy pulled the welding goggles from his head, revealing eyes that burned with determination. "I've spent my whole life taking things apart and putting them back together. Fixing what others throw away. I can't fix my childhood without him, but I can fix this. I can bring him home."

Something shifted in Juno's expression—a flicker of

recognition, perhaps even respect.

"You remind me of him," Juno muttered, sinking back into his chair. "Same stubborn streak. Same fire." He sighed deeply, shoulders slumping. "Fine. I'll tell you what I know. But that s all I'm offering."

Cristen's face brightened. "That's all we're asking."

"No, it's not," Juno replied sharply. "You want me to help you build a combat robot. To teach you how to win. But I can't."

Billy frowned. "Can't or won't?"

"Both." Juno gestured around the cave. "Look around you. I live in a hole in the ground. I don't have the necessary components to build a tournament-grade combat robot. My last machine was dismantled years ago."

"But you know how to build one," Billy pressed.

"Knowledge isn t enough. You need a power source that can sustain the kind of output required for Zoltar's arena. Those aren't exactly lying around in scrap heaps." Juno's eyes narrowed. "The kind of core you'd need is heavily regulated. Military grade. The sort of thing Zoltar keeps locked away for his champions."

"So it's impossible," Cristen said, deflating.

"I didn't say that." Juno leaned forward. "I said I don't have what you need. But that doesn't mean it doesn't exist."

Juno's expression shifted, his eyes growing distant as if recalling something from long ago. He leaned closer to the fire, his voice dropping to just above a whisper.

"There is one possibility, though most consider it nothing but old engineer's tales." He glanced over his shoulder, a habit formed from years of paranoia. "Have you ever heard of the Order of the Golden Node?"

Billy shook his head, but Cristen's eyes widened slightly.

"My grandmother used to tell stories about them," she

said. "Some kind of secret society?"

Juno nodded. "That's what the stories say. A brotherhood of scientists who discovered—or created—a power source unlike anything the world had seen before. They called it the Golden Node."

Billy leaned forward eagerly. "What kind of power source?"

"The kind that could run a thousand combat robots without depleting," Juno replied. "Free energy, limitless power—the stuff of legends. The stories claim the Node never runs out, never degrades."

"That's impossible," Billy said, though his eyes gleamed with interest.

"So is a lot of what Zoltar's accomplished," Juno countered. "The line between impossible and undiscovered gets thinner every year."

Cristen frowned. "But if this Node is so powerful, why doesn't everyone know about it? Why isn't Zoltar using it?"

"Because the Order protects it," Juno said. "Supposedly, they're a fierce group of dangerous scientists who've dedicated themselves to keeping the Node hidden. Some say they're more myth than reality—fairy tales passed down through generations of engineers to give them hope that something exists beyond corporate control."

"Do you believe they're real?" Billy asked.

Juno shrugged, poking at the fire with a metal rod. "I've never seen proof either way. But I've heard whispers, even in Zoltar's compound. His researchers were always hunting for alternative power sources. The Node came up in hushed conversations."

"So you don't know if they actually exist," Billy said, disappointment creeping into his voice.

"No," Juno admitted. "But if they do—if the Node is real—it would solve your power problem. One fragment of the Node could fuel a combat robot powerful enough to win the tournament ten times over."

Billy's fingers drummed against his tool belt, the rhythm matching his racing thoughts. "If this Node exists, how would we even find it? Where would we start looking?"

"That's the problem," Juno said, tossing another piece of scrap onto the fire. "The Order has remained hidden for generations. They don't exactly advertise their location."

Cristen tucked a strand of raven hair behind her ear. "But there must be clues, right? Stories about where they might be?"

Juno hesitated, then reached beneath his makeshift bed of salvaged cushions. He pulled out a battered metal box, its surface etched with intricate geometric patterns. The lock clicked open at his touch.

"When I escaped Zoltar's compound, I took something with me." He withdrew a yellowed piece of parchment, carefully unfolding it. "This map belonged to one of Zoltar's researchers—a man obsessed with finding the Order. He disappeared three days after I stole this."

Billy and Cristen crowded around as Juno spread the map on the ground. It showed the city and surrounding territories, with faded notations and strange symbols marking several locations. One area was circled repeatedly in red ink.

"The Northern Mountains," Billy whispered, tracing the circle with his finger.

"That's where the researcher believed the Order's sanctuary was hidden," Juno confirmed. "Deep within the mountain range, protected by natural barriers and, if the stories are true, advanced security systems."

"The Northern Mountains are at least two days' journey," Cristen said, frowning.

"We'd have to leave immediately," Billy nodded, already calculating. "If we found the Order, convinced them to help us..."

"Slow down," Juno warned. "You're assuming they'd welcome you with open arms. The Order has protected their secret for centuries. They're not going to hand over a piece of the Node to the first kid who knocks on their door."

"But my father—"

"Your father's situation might not matter to them," Juno said bluntly. "The Node is bigger than any one person."

Billy's jaw set stubbornly. "We have to try. This might be our only chance."

Juno's expression hardened as he rolled up the map with careful precision. "Listen to me very carefully, boy. If the Order is real—and that's still a big if—they aren't some friendly group of scientists waiting to help lost children."

"What do you mean?" Billy asked, his enthusiasm dimming at Juno's grave tone.

"The stories say they're killers," Juno said flatly. "Dangerous men who've eliminated anyone who's come close to discovering their secret. Engineers, explorers, even government officials—all vanished without a trace after pursuing the Node."

Cristen shifted uncomfortably. "That sounds like propaganda. Maybe Zoltar spread those rumors to keep people away."

"Maybe," Juno conceded. "But I've known men—brilliant, cautious men—who went looking for the Order and never returned." He fixed Billy with an intense stare. "One night in Zoltar's compound, I overheard two senior researchers talking. One had found evidence of the Order's sanctuary. Three days later, they found his body in his quarters. No marks, no signs of struggle. Just... dead."

Billy swallowed hard. "How do you know the Order was responsible?"

"I don't. Not for certain." Juno leaned forward, firelight casting deep shadows across his face. "But the stories are consistent. The Order protects the Node at all costs. They've supposedly developed weapons and defenses beyond anything in Zoltar's arsenal. Some say they've even found ways to extend their own lives through technology, becoming something not quite human anymore."

"You're trying to scare us," Billy said, though his voice lacked conviction.

"I'm trying to prepare you," Juno corrected. "If you're determined to find them, you need to understand what you might be walking into. These aren't kindly old professors who'll be charmed by your quest to save your father. They're guardians of perhaps the most powerful energy source on the planet, and they've kept it hidden for generations."

Cristen placed a hand on Billy's arm. "Maybe we should reconsider. Find another way."

"There is no other way," Billy said quietly, though his earlier confidence had clearly been shaken. "Not in the time we have."

Juno sighed, running a hand through his tangled hair. "If you're dead set on this madness, at least let me give you something that might help." He rummaged through a pile of salvaged items near his sleeping area and produced a small metallic disc, no larger than a pocket watch.

"What is it?" Billy asked, accepting the device.

"A frequency scanner. I built it years ago, before I swore off technology." Juno's fingers traced the worn edge with something like regret. "The Order supposedly uses unique communication signals. This might help you detect them if you get close enough."

Billy turned the device over in his hands. Despite its age, the craftsmanship was impeccable. "Thank you."

"Don't thank me for sending you to your death," Juno muttered. "The Northern Mountains are treacherous even without factoring in a secret society of murderous scientists."

Cristen studied the map again. "We'll need supplies. And a way to get there quickly."

"The transport trains run north, but they're heavily monitored," Billy said, his mind already working through the logistics. "We'd need to find another way."

Juno reached back into his box and withdrew a small key. "There's an old maintenance tunnel that leads to a garage on the outskirts of the scrapyard. I've kept a vehicle there —just in case." His expression darkened. "Never thought I'd have a reason to use it."

"You're giving us your escape plan?" Cristen asked, surprised.

"I'm giving you a fighting chance," Juno corrected. "The vehicle has enough range to get you to the mountains. After that, you're on your own."

Billy tucked the frequency scanner into his tool belt. "What made you change your mind? About helping us?"

Juno was quiet for a long moment, staring into the flames. "Your father was the only person who tried to help me escape. He created a distraction that allowed me to slip past the guards." He looked up, his eyes haunted. "I've been hiding ever since, while he remained a prisoner.

Perhaps it's time I repaid that debt."

Juno hesitated, then gestured toward the back of the cave. "There's something else I should show you."

He led them deeper into the cavern, past his living quarters and through a narrow passage that opened into a larger chamber. Flipping a switch, a series of salvaged lights flickered to life, illuminating what the darkness had concealed.

Billy's breath caught in his throat.

A massive robot chassis dominated the space, partially assembled but unmistakably built for combat. Standing nearly twelve feet tall, its frame was sleek yet formidable, with reinforced joints and specialized mounting points for weaponry. The torso was open, revealing an empty power core chamber large enough to house a substantial energy source.

"Is that—" Billy whispered, stepping forward in awe.

"The Reckoner," Juno said, his voice tinged with both pride and regret. "My final design. The one I never got to complete."

Cristen circled the machine, her green eyes wide. "You built this down here?"

"No." Juno ran his hand along the chassis's scarred shoulder plate. "I designed it in Zoltar's compound, but kept the blueprints hidden. When I escaped, I couldn't leave it behind—not after everything I'd put into it. So I disassembled it, smuggled out the parts piece by piece over months."

Billy examined the intricate wiring and custom-fabricated components. "This is incredible engineering."

"It was meant to be my masterpiece," Juno said. "The perfect balance of offense and defense, speed and power. But without a suitable energy core, it's just an empty shell."

He turned to Billy, something shifting in his expression. "If you manage to find the Order—if you somehow convince them to share even a fragment of the Node—this chassis is yours."

"Mine?" Billy's voice cracked.

"For the tournament. To save your father." Juno gestured around the cave. "I've collected additional parts over the years. Weapons systems, mobility enhancements, sensor arrays. Everything except the power source."

He placed a heavy hand on Billy's shoulder. "You'll need a proper workshop to complete it, but the foundation is solid. And you're welcome back here, to this cave, to work on it—if you return from the mountains."

Billy stared at the machine, seeing not just metal and circuitry, but possibility. Hope.

"Thank you," he said quietly.

Juno stepped back from the robot chassis, his eyes lingering on its unfinished form. A thought seemed to strike him, and he turned to Billy with sudden urgency.

"Before you go—your Cardano wallet. Is it active?"

Billy's brow furrowed in confusion. "My what?"

"Your blockchain wallet. The decentralized storage system." Juno's fingers twitched impatiently. "Your father would have set one up for you. Probably linked to your genetic signature or retinal pattern."

"I... I don't know," Billy admitted. "I've never heard of it."

Juno muttered something under his breath. "Check your father's workshop when you return home. There should be a scanner—looks like an old camera lens with a blue rim. That's the access point."

"What's this about?" Cristen asked.

"Insurance," Juno replied. "I've stored hundreds of

combat robot blueprints on-chain over the years. Technical specifications, weapon systems, defensive countermeasures—everything I designed while working for Zoltar and after my escape." His eyes met Billy's. "I've encoded them to transfer to your wallet when activated. They'll be waiting for you when you return."

"If we return," Billy said quietly.

"When," Juno corrected firmly. "I didn't survive Zoltar's compound by being pessimistic." He reached into his pocket and produced a small data chip. "This contains the access protocols. It'll help you retrieve the blueprints once you've activated the wallet."

Billy accepted the chip, tucking it carefully into an inner pocket of his jacket. "Thank you. For everything."

Juno nodded stiffly, uncomfortable with the gratitude. "The Order won't be easy to find, and they'll be even harder to convince. But if anyone has a chance..." He trailed off, then straightened his shoulders. "Good luck in your search. I hope you find what you're looking for."

"We will," Billy said with quiet determination. "And when we do, we'll come back for the Reckoner."

"I'll be here," Juno replied. "Hiding in my hole, waiting to see if fairy tales can come true after all."

CHAPTER 8: ARENA OF DREAMS

Billy and Cristen emerged from the cave entrance, squinting as their eyes adjusted to the daylight. The glaring sun cast long shadows across the scrapyard, highlighting the silhouette of a figure sitting atop a rusted droid chassis.

Relson.

His shoulders were hunched, knees pulled to his chest, eyes fixed on the ground. When he heard their footsteps crunching across the metallic debris, his head snapped up. Relief flooded his face before quickly hardening into practiced indifference.

"Thought you two got eaten or something," he muttered, sliding down from his perch.

Cristen crossed her arms. "Nice of you to wait after abandoning us."

"I didn't—" Relson started, then stopped. His gaze dropped. "Whatever."

Billy approached him, tools jangling in his belt. "The Caveman—Juno—he's going to help us. Sort of."

"Great." Relson kicked at a small gear. "Glad your little chat went well after I..."

"Ran away?" Cristen supplied.

Relson's face flushed red. "You would've too if you'd seen what I've seen in these scrapyards. People disappear here all the time."

"So why'd you wait?" Billy asked quietly.

The question caught Relson off guard. He opened his mouth, closed it, then shrugged with forced casualness. "Figured someone needed to pull your sorry butts out if things went south."

"While hiding safely outside," Cristen noted.

"Look, I'm not like you two, okay?" Relson's voice cracked slightly. "I don't have fancy tech skills or big brains. I just... I just know how to survive."

Billy studied him for a moment. "Surviving isn't the same as living, though."

"What's that supposed to mean?"

"It means sometimes you have to risk something to gain something." Billy gestured back toward the cave. "Juno's been surviving down there for years, but he's not really living. He's just... existing."

Relson scuffed his boot against the ground. "So I'm a coward. Is that what you're saying?"

"No," Billy said. "I'm saying next time, we stick together. All of us. Because that's how we'll do more than just survive."

A beat of silence passed between them.

"So," Relson finally said, straightening his shoulders. "What's the plan now?"

A mechanical whirring cut through the air, growing louder as a small yellow blur zipped around a mountain of scrap metal. Zippy darted erratically between piles of discarded robot parts, his antenna twitching frantically.

"There you are," Billy said, relief washing over his face.

Zippy hovered in front of the group, emitting a series of indignant chirps and beeps.

"I didn't leave you behind on purpose," Billy translated for the others. "You were recharging."

The little drone bobbed up and down aggressively, its mechanical arms gesticulating wildly.

"What's it saying?" Relson asked, eyeing the agitated machine.

"He's upset because I didn't wake him up before we left," Billy explained. "Says he could've helped navigate the cave system."

Zippy circled Billy's head, letting out a staccato of beeps that sounded remarkably like scolding.

"Looks like someone's in the doghouse," Cristen smirked.

The drone swooped down to face Billy directly, its glowing eyes intensifying as it emitted a longer, more complex series of sounds.

Billy's eyebrows shot up. "No, I promise I won't do it again."

More beeping.

"Yes, even if you're recharging."

Zippy's mechanical arms crossed in front of its body, somehow conveying profound skepticism.

"Look," Billy said, reaching up to pat the drone. "We're a team, right? I shouldn't have left without you. Won't happen again."

The drone hovered silently for a moment before emitting a softer, accepting chirp. Then it flew in a quick circle around the group, as if taking inventory of everyone present.

"What's it doing now?" Relson asked.

"Scanning everyone," Billy explained. "He's making sure we're all okay after being in the cave."

Zippy completed his circuit and returned to hover by Billy's shoulder, letting out a satisfied beep.

"Well, now that the family reunion's over," Relson said,

"can we get back to figuring out our next move?"

Billy pulled out his father's schematics, the weathered paper crinkling as he unfolded it on top of a flat piece of scrap metal. Zippy hovered overhead, projecting a soft light onto the blueprint.

"So here's where we stand," Billy said, tapping the diagram. "Juno told us about the Order of the Golden Node. They might be our best shot at finding a power source for the Reckoner."

"The what now?" Relson leaned in, squinting at the complex design.

"The Reckoner," Billy repeated, his finger tracing the outline of a combat robot chassis. "My father's ultimate design. If we can build this, we've got a real chance at the tournament."

Cristen nodded. "According to Juno, the Order operates somewhere in the Northern Mountains. They're tech purists who believe in using technology responsibly."

"Or they're dangerous fanatics," Relson countered. "That's what you said the Caveman told you, right?"

"He wasn't sure," Billy admitted. "But they're the only lead we have for finding a power cell strong enough for this design."

Relson studied the blueprint, his eyes widening slightly. "This thing looks... serious. Like, military-grade serious."

"That's why we need that power source," Cristen said. "Nothing conventional will do."

Relson ran his hand through his hair, considering. "Look, this Order sounds sketchy, and the Northern Mountains is no joke. Automated security, rival scavengers, the works."

Billy's face fell. "So you're bailing again?"

"No," Relson said firmly. "I'm saying I should stay

here. These schematics need parts, right? Specialized components?"

Billy nodded slowly.

"I know this scrapyard better than anyone," Relson continued. "While you two track down this Order, I can gather what we need to actually build this thing once you get the power source."

Cristen and Billy exchanged surprised looks.

"You'd do that?" Billy asked.

Relson shrugged, but there was determination in his eyes. "Consider it making up for the whole running away thing. Besides, I've got contacts with other scavengers. I can find stuff you'd never locate on your own."

"That... actually makes sense," Cristen admitted.

"I know my strengths," Relson said. "And right now, they're more useful here than trailing you two into some tech cult's territory."

Billy looked at the scattered robotic parts surrounding them. "Relson, I need you to do more than just find parts. Take everything useful you collect and bring it to Juno's cave."

"The cave?" Relson's eyes widened. "You want me to go back in there? With the crazy hermit?"

"He's not crazy," Billy said, adjusting his welding goggles. "Just... isolated. And his cave is the perfect workshop—hidden, spacious, and Juno knows more about combat robots than anyone else alive."

Cristen nodded. "Plus, it's safer than leaving valuable parts lying around where anyone could steal them."

Relson kicked at a small servo motor half-buried in the dirt. "What if he doesn't want me barging in with armfuls of junk?"

"Already cleared it with him," Billy said. "He's not thrilled, but he agreed. Said something about 'keeping an eye on the operation' and 'making sure we don't repeat past mistakes.'"

Zippy chirped enthusiastically, circling around Relson's head before projecting a holographic map of the cave system onto the ground between them.

"Whoa," Relson muttered, crouching to examine the detailed projection. "Your little flying trash can is actually pretty useful."

Zippy made an indignant beeping sound.

"He doesn't like being called that," Billy translated with a smirk. "But yeah, he mapped the entire cave while we were talking to Juno. This main chamber here—" he pointed to the largest hollow on the map "—that's where you should store everything."

"And what exactly am I looking for?" Relson asked.

Billy pulled a small data chip from his tool belt and handed it to Relson. "This has the complete parts list. Zippy, give him a copy of the schematics."

The drone projected the robot design onto Relson's palm, highlighting various components in different colors.

"Red items are critical," Billy explained. "Yellow are important but we can improvise if necessary. Green are nice-to-haves."

Relson studied the projection, nodding slowly. "Some of this stuff is rare, but I know where to look. The military surplus pile on the east side might have those actuators."

"Just be careful," Cristen warned. "And don't try to carry too much at once. Make multiple trips if you have to."

"And Relson?" Billy added, his voice serious. "If Juno offers any advice about the parts, listen to him. He's forgotten more about combat robots than most engineers will ever know."

Relson pocketed the data chip with surprising care. "I've got this. Just don't get yourselves killed chasing fairy tales in the mountains."

"We won't," Billy promised, already calculating their journey in his head. "Cristen and I will head out at dawn tomorrow. The sooner we find the Order, the sooner we can start building."

The afternoon sun cast long shadows across the scrapyard as they finalized their plans. Zippy hovered nearby, occasionally projecting updated maps and schematics when needed.

"One more thing," Billy said, reaching into his tool belt. He pulled out a small communicator, its casing scratched but functional. "Take this. It's paired with Zippy's systems. If you find something important or run into trouble, we can stay in touch."

Relson took the device, turning it over in his hands. "This range can't possibly reach the Northern Mountains."

"It doesn't need to," Billy explained. "Zippy can relay the signal through various communication towers. As long as we're both within range of some kind of network, we can connect."

"Clever," Relson admitted, clipping the communicator to his belt.

As they prepared to part ways, Cristen pulled something from her pocket—a small, intricately carved wooden token. She pressed it into Relson's palm.

"What's this for?" he asked, examining the strange symbols etched into its surface.

"Luck," she said simply. "My mother gave it to me when I was little. Said it would protect me when I ventured into unknown territory." She shrugged, suddenly self-conscious. "Figured you might need it more than me right now."

Relson stared at the token, clearly caught off guard by the gesture. "I'll... I'll keep it safe," he managed, tucking it securely in an inner pocket.

Billy checked his watch. "We should head back. Got supplies to pack if we're leaving at dawn."

The three stood in awkward silence for a moment, none quite knowing how to say goodbye when so much uncertainty lay ahead.

The walk back to Billy's house was quiet, each lost in their thoughts about the journey ahead. The neighborhood streets were bathed in the golden hues of late afternoon as they approached the modest dwelling Billy called home.

"You really think this Order exists?" Cristen asked, breaking the silence.

Billy adjusted his welding goggles atop his head. "Has to. The power requirements for the Reckoner are off the charts. Nothing conventional will work."

"And if they're dangerous like Juno warned?"

"Then we'll figure something out. We always do."

Inside Billy's house, they headed straight for his room. Zippy darted ahead, circling the ceiling before settling on a small charging pad in the corner. The drone's eyes dimmed slightly as it began downloading geographical data for their journey.

Billy pulled out an old canvas backpack from under his bed. The fabric was worn but sturdy, reinforced with metal strips along the seams—one of his earlier modifications. He began methodically sorting through his tool collection, selecting only the essentials.

"Water purification tablets," Cristen said, placing a small container on the bed. "My dad always says you can survive

without food but not without clean water."
Billy nodded, adding them to the growing pile. "Good thinking."
Cristen watched as he carefully packed a compact multi-tool, wire cutters, and a set of precision screwdrivers. "You're bringing a lot of tech for someone hunting down tech purists."
"Know your audience," Billy replied with a shrug. "If these people respect technology like Juno says, showing up with quality tools might earn their respect."
He hesitated over a small device with a cracked display. "My first circuit tester. Dad gave it to me when I was five."
"Sentimental value won't help if it doesn't work," Cristen said gently.
"Yeah." Billy set it aside reluctantly. "You're right."
Cristen pulled her tech bow from her shoulder, checking its mechanisms. "This needs a full charge before we leave. Think your mom will mind if I plug in?"
"She'll be at work until late. Help yourself."
As Cristen connected her weapon to the charging station, she noticed Billy staring at his father's old workshop blueprints.
"We're going to find him," she said softly.
"I know." Billy carefully folded the blueprint and tucked it into a waterproof sleeve. "But first, we need that power source."
As the evening deepened outside, Billy and Cristen continued their preparations. The mechanical whir of Zippy's charging station provided a comforting background noise as they sorted through supplies.
Billy paused, a handful of spare batteries clutched in his palm. He watched Cristen methodically checking her tech bow's calibration, her brow furrowed in concentration.

"You know," he said quietly, "you don't have to come with me."

Cristen looked up, her green eyes reflecting the room's soft light. "What?"

"The Northern Mountains, the Order, all of it. It's dangerous, and it's my father, not yours." Billy set the batteries down. "You could stay here, help Relson gather parts. Probably safer."

"Is that what you want?"

Billy shook his head. "No. But I'd understand if—"

"Then stop talking nonsense." She returned to adjusting her bow.

A small smile tugged at the corner of Billy's mouth. "I've never actually thanked you, have I?"

"For what?"

"For sticking with me through all this." Billy gestured vaguely around the room, at the scattered tools and half-finished inventions. "Most people think I'm just the weird kid who talks to machines."

Cristen snorted. "You are the weird kid who talks to machines."

"See? That's what I mean." Billy's smile widened. "Anyone else would've said that to hurt me. You say it like it's just... me."

She shrugged, but her expression softened. "That's because it is just you. And there's nothing wrong with that."

Billy fiddled with a screwdriver, turning it over in his hands. "I don't know what I'd do without you, Cristen. You've been there through everything—when kids at school called me names, when I blew up half the science lab with that faulty capacitor—"

"That was actually pretty funny after the smoke cleared."

"—and now you're about to trek into the mountains to help me find my dad." Billy looked up, meeting her eyes. "I just... I'm really grateful to have a friend like you. Someone who gets it. Gets me."

Cristen's cheeks flushed slightly. She looked down, adjusting a strap on her bow that didn't need adjusting. "Yeah, well. Someone has to keep you from blowing yourself up permanently."

The silence between them settled comfortably as they continued packing. Zippy chirped from its charging station, a series of beeps that made Billy laugh.

"What'd it say?" Cristen asked.

"Says we should bring extra socks. Apparently the weather data for the Northern Mountains shows frequent rain this time of year."

"Smart little trash can," she muttered, then quickly added, "Don't tell it I said that."

Billy zipped up his backpack, testing its weight. "I think we're as ready as we'll ever be."

A soft knock at the bedroom door made them both turn. Billy's mother stood in the doorway, her expression a careful mask that didn't quite hide her concern.

"I made some sandwiches," she said, holding up a plate. "Thought you might be hungry with all this... planning."

Billy and Cristen exchanged glances.

"Thanks, Mom," Billy said, taking the plate.

She lingered, eyes moving over the packed bags and equipment. "So. The Northern Mountains."

Billy froze mid-bite. "You heard?"

"These walls aren't exactly soundproof, honey." She sighed, leaning against the doorframe. "I knew this would happen eventually. Ever since you found that message from your father."

"Mom, I have to—"

She held up her hand. "I know. You're your father's son in every way." A sad smile crossed her face. "Including the stubborn streak."

Billy set down his sandwich. "You're not going to try to stop me?"

"Would it work?" When Billy shook his head, she continued, "Then I'd rather help you than fight you.

CHAPTER 9: ALLOY AND AMBITION

Billy adjusted his welding goggles as they ascended the narrow mountain path. Three days of travel had brought them deep into the Northern Mountains, where jagged peaks pierced the clouds and the air grew thin and cold.

"The coordinates from my father's notes should be just ahead," Billy said, checking the small device in his palm.

Cristen moved ahead, bow at the ready. "Something's not right. These rocks—they're too uniform."

Billy ran his gloved hand along the stone face. "You're right. These aren't natural formations."

They rounded a bend and froze. Before them stood an enormous stone archway, half-collapsed and covered in moss and lichen. Ancient symbols lined its edges, faded but still visible.

"Hidden in plain sight," Billy whispered.

Inside, the passage opened to a vast chamber, illuminated by strange bioluminescent fungi clinging to the ceiling. The walls were covered with intricate diagrams—circuitry patterns, mechanical designs, and symbols neither had seen before.

"It's like a technological temple," Cristen said, running her fingers over the engravings.

Billy examined a circular depression in the center of the floor. "Look at this pattern. It's a locking mechanism."

He pulled out his father's blueprint and compared the designs. "These match! Dad must have been here."

They spent hours navigating the ruins, solving mechanical puzzles that opened new passages. One required aligning reflective panels to direct light beams. Another involved arranging gears in a specific sequence to unlock a massive stone door.

"Whoever built this didn't want just anyone getting through," Cristen said, wiping sweat from her brow despite the chill.

In the final chamber, they faced a wall covered in mathematical equations. Billy's eyes widened as he recognized his father's handwriting among the ancient symbols.

"He added to their work," Billy muttered, tracing the equations. "The solution is here somewhere."

After several failed attempts, Billy arranged a sequence of symbols in the correct order. A low rumbling shook the chamber, and a section of the wall slid away.

"We did it!" Cristen exclaimed.

But their excitement quickly faded. The opening revealed was barely larger than Zippy—a narrow tunnel that no human could possibly fit through.

"All this way for... this?" Cristen stared at the tiny passageway.

Billy knelt before the opening, shining his light into the darkness beyond. "It's not the end. It's just not meant for us."

The ground beneath them trembled. Dust rained from the ceiling as a magnified voice boomed through the chamber, reverberating off every surface.

"WHO DARES TRESPASS ON THE SACRED GROUNDS OF THE NODE?"

Billy stumbled backward, colliding with Cristen. Zippy darted behind Billy's shoulder, chirping frantically.

"The—the voice is coming from everywhere," Cristen whispered, her bow half-raised but with no clear target.

The voice thundered again. "IDENTIFY YOURSELVES OR FACE THE CONSEQUENCES OF YOUR INTRUSION."

Billy swallowed hard, then stepped forward. "My name is Billy Applebaum. This is my friend Cristen and my drone Zippy."

"AND WHAT BRINGS YOU TO THIS FORBIDDEN PLACE, BILLY APPLEBAUM?"

Billy pulled his father's message device from his pocket. "I'm looking for answers about my father, Melvin Applebaum. He disappeared years ago. His notes led us here."

Silence followed, stretching uncomfortably long.

"We need help," Cristen added, lowering her bow completely. "Billy's father was taken by Zoltar. We believe he knew about this place—about the Node. We're trying to build a combat robot to enter Zoltar's tournament, but we need a power source."

"Please," Billy said. "My father might have been here. He left coordinates, designs. I just want to find him."

The voice returned, softer now but still commanding. "APPLEBAUM. YES. THE ENGINEER WHO SOUGHT KNOWLEDGE WITHOUT SEEKING POWER. HE CAME HERE ONCE."

Billy's eyes widened. "You knew my father? Is he—"

"HE LEFT LONG AGO. BUT HIS RESPECT FOR THE NODE'S POWER WAS... UNCOMMON."

The chamber fell silent. Billy and Cristen exchanged uncertain glances.

"What do we—" Cristen began, but her words were cut

short.

A brilliant golden light erupted from the small tunnel entrance, engulfing them in a pulsating glow. Billy felt a strange tingling sensation spread through his body, starting at his fingertips and racing up his arms. The sensation wasn't painful, but it felt like every atom in his body was vibrating at an impossible frequency.

"Zippy!" Billy called out as the drone spiraled in the air, caught in the same golden energy.

The world around them began to shift. The stone walls seemed to stretch upward, growing impossibly tall. The ceiling receded into darkness. Billy blinked rapidly, trying to clear his vision, but the distortion continued.

"What's happening?" Cristen's voice sounded oddly distant.

Billy looked down at his hands. They appeared normal, but the tools on his belt now seemed oversized, as if designed for someone much larger. That's when the realization hit him.

"We're shrinking," he whispered.

The golden light intensified for a moment before fading. When it cleared, Billy staggered backward, disoriented. The chamber they stood in was now colossal. The ceiling towered hundreds of feet above them. The symbols on the walls were now massive carvings, each one taller than Billy himself.

Zippy buzzed around them, chirping in confusion. The drone seemed to be the only thing that had remained the same size.

"It's not the room that's bigger," Cristen said, her voice shaking slightly. "It's us that's smaller."

Billy turned toward what had been the tiny tunnel entrance. What was once barely large enough for Zippy now stood as a grand archway, perfectly sized for them to walk through.

The voice returned, now sounding less booming and more like a normal, elderly man. "THE PATH IS OPEN TO THOSE WHO SEEK KNOWLEDGE WITHOUT DESTRUCTION. PROCEED, CHILDREN OF APPLEBAUM."

Billy took a tentative step toward the archway. "I think we're supposed to go through."

Cristen nodded, still looking stunned. "This is... impossible."

"Yet here we are." Billy gestured toward the now-accessible passage. "Ready?"

The passage widened as they ventured deeper, revealing walls lined with glowing circuitry that pulsed with golden energy. Billy ran his fingers along the patterns, recognizing elements from his father's blueprints.

"It's like walking through a living machine," he whispered.

After several minutes, the tunnel opened into a vast chamber that defied comprehension. The ceiling arched hundreds of feet above them, supported by columns of translucent material that seemed to shift between solid and liquid states. In the center, suspended in midair, hovered a small golden orb no larger than a marble, radiating waves of energy that rippled outward like water.

"The Node," Billy breathed.

Around the chamber, a dozen elderly figures in green robes worked at holographic interfaces or tended to machinery Billy couldn't begin to understand. Their movements were deliberate, almost ritualistic. Most striking were the cybernetic enhancements visible beneath their robes—silver limbs, glowing blue optical implants, tubes connecting to canisters on their backs.

As Billy and Cristen stepped forward, the elders turned in unison. Their expressions hardened.

"Intruders," one of them said, his voice crackling with age and static. "How did they find this place?"

Another raised a mechanical arm that transformed into what looked like a weapon. "They must not be allowed near the Node."

Zippy chirped nervously, hovering close to Billy's shoulder.

"Wait," Billy said, raising his hands. "We're not here to cause trouble. My father—"

"Silence!" A commanding voice cut through the chamber. The elders parted as another figure approached. Unlike the others, this one walked with a cane, his back slightly hunched. His face was hidden behind ancient welding goggles that seemed permanently fused to his skin. The cannister on his back hovered independently, connected to his body by a series of tubes.

"I am Eek, Guardian of the Node," he announced. "And you are trespassers in our sacred temple."

Cristen stepped forward. "We followed coordinates left by Melvin Applebaum. We need help."

Eek's expression remained impassive. "Applebaum. That name has not been spoken here in many cycles." He circled them slowly, examining them with evident suspicion. "His son, perhaps? You have his eyes."

"Yes," Billy replied. "He's been captured by Zoltar. We need a power source for a combat robot to enter the tournament and save him."

Murmurs rippled through the gathered elders. Eek raised his hand for silence.

"The Node is not a battery for children's toys," he said

coldly. "Many have sought our power. All have been denied."

"With all due respect," Billy said, his voice steadier than he felt, "this isn't about a toy. It's about saving my father from a man who would use your power for destruction."

Eek tapped his cane against the floor. "Bold words from one so young. What makes you think you're worthy of the Node's power when so many have been turned away?"

Billy unclipped his tool belt and set it carefully on the ground. "May I?" he asked, gesturing toward a nearby console that was emitting a discordant hum.

The elders exchanged glances. Eek nodded once, skepticism evident in his posture.

Billy approached the console, examining the holographic displays. "Your harmonic stabilizer is out of alignment. The frequency modulation is cycling too rapidly."

Zippy hovered nearby, chirping a series of tones. Billy nodded. "You're right, Zippy. The quantum flux is oscillating at 0.03 hertz above optimal."

Without waiting for permission, Billy's hands moved across the interface. His fingers danced through the holographic controls with practiced precision, adjusting parameters and realigning systems.

"The problem is here," he explained, pointing to a section of the display. "Your primary resonance chamber is compensating for a degraded tertiary coil. If you keep running it this way, you'll burn out the entire eastern grid within three cycles."

One of the elders stepped forward. "Impossible. How could a child possibly—"

The discordant hum suddenly shifted, harmonizing into a perfect tone. The golden light throughout the chamber brightened noticeably.

"I didn't fix it," Billy said, stepping back. "Just stabilized it temporarily. The tertiary coil needs physical replacement, not just recalibration."

Eek moved closer, examining the console. "Interesting. Where did you learn such skills?"

"I taught myself. Mostly from taking things apart and putting them back together." Billy smiled gently trying to hide his pride.

The drone performed a small aerial loop, as if showing off.

Eek studied Billy with newfound interest. "You have your father's talent. Perhaps more." He turned to the other elders. "Impressive, but technical skill alone does not earn our trust. The Node's power is not given lightly."

Eek tapped his cane three times on the floor. The sound echoed unnaturally, and the chamber transformed around them. The walls receded into darkness, and the Node itself dimmed until it was barely visible.

"The power you seek is not merely energy," Eek said. "It is consciousness. Wisdom. To wield it requires more than technical skill. It requires understanding."

Three pedestals rose from the floor, each bearing a strange crystalline device.

"Each of you must face the Node's judgment," Eek continued. "The boy, the girl, and even your mechanical companion."

Billy approached the first pedestal cautiously. "What do we have to do?"

"Place your hand upon the crystal. The Node will see into your mind—your fears, your desires, your true intentions."

Billy hesitated, then placed his palm on the cool surface. The crystal flared with golden light, and Billy gasped. His eyes went wide, unfocused, seeing something beyond the physical world.

In his mind, Billy stood in Zoltar's arena. Before him lay the broken remains of his combat robot. Zoltar laughed from his elevated platform, holding his father captive. "You failed," the vision-Zoltar mocked. "Just like your father failed. All that knowledge, and you couldn't save him."

Billy felt rage build inside him. The vision shifted, showing him at the controls of a massive war machine powered by the Node, laying waste to Zoltar's compound, heedless of the innocent lives caught in the destruction.

"Is this what you truly want?" Eek's voice echoed in his mind. "Power without restraint? Vengeance without mercy?"

Billy struggled internally. "No," he finally answered. "I want justice, not revenge. I want to save my father, not become like Zoltar."

The vision faded, replaced by another—Billy using his knowledge to build, to heal, to protect. Creating machines that helped rather than destroyed.

The crystal dimmed, and Billy staggered back, breathing heavily.

"You faced your darkest impulse," Eek said, "and chose a better path."

Cristen approached her crystal next, while Zippy hovered over the third. Each underwent their own trial, facing fears and temptations unique to them.

When all three had completed their tests, Eek nodded solemnly. "The Node has judged you worthy—not because you are perfect, but because you recognize your imperfections. You seek power not for its own sake, but for something greater."

As they moved deeper into the temple complex, Billy noticed something odd about the other inhabitants. Scattered among the elders were younger people tending gardens, repairing equipment, or simply going about daily life. Something about them seemed familiar.

"Wait," Billy whispered to Cristen, grabbing her arm. "Isn't that Professor Kline? The robotics expert who disappeared three years ago?"

Cristen squinted at a middle-aged woman adjusting a hydroponics system. "You're right. And over there—that's Joanna Wei! She was a quantum physicist who vanished during an expedition last year. My mom had her picture on our fridge for months."

Billy scanned the chamber, recognizing more faces. "They're all here. People who were reported missing..."

Eek nodded, tapping his cane against the floor. "Observant. Yes, many who were thought lost to the outside world have found purpose here."

"But why?" Cristen asked. "Why disappear from their lives?"

A woman approached—Professor Kline herself. "Because here, we can do what was impossible out there." She gestured around them. "At our reduced size, resources that were scarce become abundant. A single apple can feed twenty. A drop of water sustains many."

"We live in harmony," added another man, whom Billy recognized as a renowned engineer. "No competition for resources, no struggle for survival. The Node provides energy without limit, without pollution."

"Those deemed worthy are offered a choice," Eek explained. "Remain in the outside world with its scarcity and conflict, or join us here, where your talents serve a greater purpose."

Billy looked around in wonder. "So you just... shrink people who deserve to be here?"

"Only those who prove themselves," Eek said. "Those who demonstrate wisdom, compassion, and respect for knowledge. The Node judges, not us."

"Your father was offered this choice," Professor Kline said softly. "He declined. He believed he could do more good in the outside world, fighting against those who would misuse technology."

Billy's eyes widened. "He knew about this place all along..."

"And protected our secret," Eek confirmed. "Even from his own family."

Eek led Billy and Cristen to a small meditation chamber away from the main hall. Glowing symbols danced across the walls, casting gentle golden shadows as they settled onto cushioned seats.

"You've heard tales of our temple, no doubt," Eek said, leaning on his cane. "Stories of death traps and vengeful guardians who vaporize intruders on sight."

Billy nodded. "The Caveman—Juno—he warned us not to come. Said the Order was dangerous."

Eek's weathered face cracked into a smile. "Good. Those stories serve their purpose well." He tapped his cane against the floor, creating a ripple of light. "We cultivate these legends deliberately. The more frightening the tales, the fewer curious treasure-hunters come seeking our power."

"You want people to be afraid of you," Cristen realized.

"Those with ill intentions are easily deterred by fear," Eek explained. "They seek power without risk, wealth without sacrifice. Our reputation keeps them at bay." His gaze settled on Billy. "But those with the purest intentions—those like your father—they come despite the warnings, willing to risk everything for something they believe in."

Billy ran his fingers along the edge of his goggles. "A test of character."

"Precisely." Eek raised his hand, and a small portion of golden light separated from his canister, hovering between them. "The Node has judged you worthy, Billy Applebaum. Not just of knowledge, but of trust."

The golden light condensed, forming a crystal no larger than Billy's thumbnail. It pulsed with inner radiance, like a heartbeat.

"A fragment of the Node," Eek said. "Small, but powerful enough to fuel your combat robot beyond anything Zoltar has ever witnessed."

Billy stared at the crystal, speechless.

"This is not a gift given lightly," Eek continued. "It comes with responsibility. Use it to save your father, not for vengeance."

"I will," Billy whispered, accepting the fragment with trembling hands.

"And know this—should you wish to join our cause someday, you will be welcome." Eek's voice softened. "But not yet. Live your life, Billy. Experience the world above. Make your own choices." He chuckled. "Wait until you're at least in your forties to decide. Youth should not be spent underground, no matter how wondrous our sanctuary."

CHAPTER 10: PULSE OF THE PAST

The return journey felt different. The path that had seemed so treacherous on their way to the Order now appeared almost welcoming, as if the mountains themselves recognized their purpose. Billy clutched the crystal fragment in his pocket, feeling its warmth pulse against his fingertips.

"You haven't said much since we left," Cristen noted as they navigated a narrow pass. Zippy flew ahead, chirping excitedly as he scouted their route.

"Just thinking about the Node, what it could mean for the Reckoner." Billy's eyes gleamed with calculation. "If I calibrate the power distribution matrix correctly, I could achieve at least three hundred percent efficiency over standard power cells. Maybe even incorporate a recursive feedback loop to—"

"Billy." Cristen stopped walking, forcing him to pause. "Is that all you got from this experience? A power source?"

"No, of course not." He blinked, confused by her tone. "But this is how we save my father."

Zippy circled back, hovering between them with a concerned series of beeps.

"You're doing it again," Cristen said, crossing her arms. "Treating this like it's just another engineering problem. Input A plus component B equals solution C."

"Isn't it?" Billy frowned. "We needed power, we found power."

"We found people, Billy. An entire community that chose connection over isolation." She gestured back toward the mountain. "They could have used that technology for anything, but they chose to create harmony."

Billy shifted uncomfortably. "What's your point?"

"My point is that your father isn't just some broken machine waiting for you to fix him." Her green eyes locked onto his. "And neither are your friends. Or your mom. Or anyone else in your life."

Zippy settled on Billy's shoulder, emitting a soft, supportive hum.

"People aren't circuit boards you can rewire when they don't behave the way you want," Cristen continued, her voice softening. "You can't just shut them down and restart when they're difficult. You have to listen. Connect."

"I know that," Billy muttered, though his eyes dropped to the ground.

"Do you? Because sometimes it feels like you're so focused on controlling every variable that you forget we're here to help, not just follow instructions."

Billy kicked at a loose stone, sending it tumbling down the path. "That s not fair. I'm trying to save my father. Everything I do is for that."

"I know." Cristen's expression softened. "But Eek was right about power without understanding. What happens after you rescue your father? Have you thought about that?"

The question hung between them. Billy hadn't considered beyond the rescue, beyond the tournament. His entire focus had been on the mechanics of the mission, not its aftermath.

"I just want my family back," he finally admitted, his voice smaller than usual.

Zippy chirped softly, his mechanical eyes dimming in sympathy.

"And you deserve that," Cristen said, stepping closer. "But don't forget to value what you already have. The connections you've made. Me, Zippy, even Relson."

Billy looked up, a reluctant smile forming. "Even Relson?"

"Even Relson," she laughed. "Though I'll deny saying that if you tell him."

They resumed walking, the tension between them easing. As they descended into familiar territory, Billy pulled out the Node fragment, studying how the afternoon light caught its golden surface.

"You know what's strange?" he said. "All my life I've been building things, taking them apart, putting them back together. But this..." He held up the fragment. "This is different. It's not just power—it's connection. Like those Elders said."

"Now you're getting it." Cristen grinned.

"Maybe I've been approaching everything wrong. Not just the Reckoner, but everything." Billy's fingers closed around the Node. "My dad wasn't just building robots. He was creating something that connected with people."

Zippy buzzed excitedly, circling their heads before darting ahead.

"Looks like someone's eager to get back to the cave," Cristen observed.

"Can't blame him. We've got work to do." Billy's pace quickened. "But this time, I think I understand what kind of work it really is."

As they neared the outskirts of the scrapyard, the

familiar silhouettes of discarded robots rose against the darkening sky. Billy felt a strange comfort in the chaos of mechanical remains—a feeling he now recognized might not be entirely healthy.

"I've been thinking about what Eek said," Billy ventured, hopping over a fallen drone chassis. "About power without understanding."

"It's not just about machines," Cristen replied, carefully picking her way through a tangle of wires. "It's about people too."

Billy nodded slowly. "All this time, I've been collecting information about my dad, about what happened to him. But information isn't the same as knowing someone, is it?"

Zippy chirped in agreement, his little lights blinking rhythmically.

"That's exactly it." Cristen stopped walking, her silhouette framed by the setting sun behind her. "You can have all the answers in the world, but without connection, they're just... data. Facts without meaning."

"Like reading a blueprint without understanding what you're building," Billy said.

"Answers without connection are just more silence." Cristen's voice was soft but firm. "That's what I've been trying to tell you. Finding your father isn't just about the physical rescue—it's about understanding who he was. Who you are because of him, and who you are without him."

Billy let her words sink in, feeling their weight settle alongside the Node fragment in his pocket. For the first time, he considered that perhaps the void he'd been trying to fill with mechanical precision couldn't be solved with perfect engineering.

"I think I get it now," he said, looking up at her. "The Node isn't just power—it's what connects everything in their community. What if that's what I've been missing? Not just with my dad, but with everyone?"

Zippy hovered closer, emitting a series of gentle beeps that Billy intuitively understood as encouragement.

"You're not alone in this, Billy," Cristen said, placing her hand on his shoulder. "That's the whole point."

The cavern transformed into an impromptu workshop over the next three days. Juno cleared a section near the eastern wall, where natural light filtered through the skylights for most of the day. Billy set up a makeshift workbench from salvaged metal sheets while Cristen organized their growing collection of parts.

"Pass me that servo actuator," Billy called from beneath the half-assembled frame of the Reckoner. His voice echoed against the cave walls as he lay on his back, welding goggles pulled down over his eyes.

Relson dragged in another haul of parts, his arms straining under the weight of a combat-grade hydraulic system. "Found this beauty in the north quadrant. Still functional."

"Perfect timing." Billy slid out from under the chassis, his face smudged with grease. "That's exactly what we need for the secondary mobility system."

Zippy hovered near the ceiling, projecting a holographic blueprint that Billy had refined based on his father's original designs. The drone chirped excitedly whenever they completed a major component.

Days blurred together. Mornings began with Juno teaching Billy combat maneuvers while Cristen and Relson sorted through scrap. Afternoons were dedicated to assembly, with all four huddled around the growing form of the Reckoner.

"The power distribution needs to be perfectly balanced," Billy explained, carefully installing the Node fragment into a custom housing he'd designed. "Too much power to the offensive systems will leave us vulnerable. Too much to defense, and we'll never land a hit."

Cristen worked alongside him, her fingers deftly connecting micro-filament wiring. "Like everything else in life," she remarked. "Balance."

Even Relson, who'd initially been clumsy with the finer technical work, developed a surprising talent for structural reinforcement. "The armor plating needs to flex here," he demonstrated, bending a sheet of metal with surprising precision. "Absorbs impact better."

By the fourth evening, the Reckoner had taken recognizable form. Its torso and limbs were assembled, though the head unit remained incomplete. The cockpit —designed for Billy to pilot from within—was functional but bare.

"It's beautiful," Cristen whispered, standing back to admire their work.

"Half-beautiful," Billy corrected, wiping his hands on a rag. "We're only halfway there."

Juno circled the robot, his experienced eyes assessing their progress. "The foundation is solid. Tomorrow we begin the real work—making this machine an extension of yourself."

Morning light sliced through the skylights, casting geometric patterns across the Reckoner's partially completed frame. Billy adjusted a power coupling, his movements precise and methodical. He'd been up since dawn, making minute calibrations to the Node fragment's housing.

"You're thinking like an engineer again," Juno said, appearing beside him with silent footsteps that belied his age.

Billy glanced up, confusion crossing his face. "I am an engineer."

"In the arena, you're a fighter first." Juno tapped the robot's chassis with his walking stick. "This isn't just a machine—it's a weapon, an extension of your will."

"But the technical specifications—"

"Mean nothing if you can't anticipate your opponent." Juno beckoned Billy away from the workbench. "Come. Leave the tools."

Reluctantly, Billy set down his calibrator and followed Juno to an open area of the cavern. Zippy trailed behind, curious.

"Close your eyes," Juno instructed. "Now, tell me—what happens when an opponent strikes from your left?"

"I'd activate the lateral shield generators and—"

"Too slow. You're dead." Juno's voice was sharp. "Don't think about what buttons to push. Feel the attack coming. React with instinct, not calculation."

Billy frowned. "But the systems need precise input to—"

"The greatest champions don't win because their robots have better parts." Juno circled Billy slowly. "They win because they understand the rhythm of combat. The psychology of their opponents."

He tapped Billy's temple. "The battle happens here first. Every move, every countermove—it's a conversation. Your father understood this."

"My father was an engineer too," Billy protested.

"Your father was a warrior who used engineering as his medium." Juno picked up two metal rods from a pile of scrap. He handed one to Billy. "Now, try to hit me."

Billy hesitated, then swung the rod awkwardly. Juno sidestepped effortlessly.

"Again."

Billy swung harder. Juno deflected the blow with his own rod, the metal singing on impact.

"You're thinking about where to strike. Stop thinking. Feel the opening."

For an hour, they continued this dance—Billy attacking, Juno evading or countering. Gradually, Billy's movements became less calculated, more fluid.

"Better," Juno said as Billy finally managed to tap him lightly on the shoulder. "You stopped trying to solve the problem and started responding to the moment."

"But how does this help with the Reckoner?"

"Because the Reckoner isn't just circuits and metal. It's you." Juno placed a hand on the robot's frame. "In the arena, competitors who treat their machines as separate from themselves always lose. Your father knew his creations as intimately as his own body."

Understanding dawned in Billy's eyes. "It's not about building the perfect robot..."

"It's about becoming the perfect team," Juno finished. "Now, let's try again. This time, imagine the rod is the Reckoner's arm. Feel its weight, its balance, its potential."

Cristen leaned against the cave wall, watching Billy and Juno spar with their makeshift staffs. Her fingers tapped rhythmically against her bow as she analyzed their movements.

"He's getting better," she remarked to Relson, who was sorting through a pile of sensor arrays.

"Still too predictable," Relson replied, holding a component up to the light. "Zoltar's fighters will eat him alive if he telegraphs his moves like that."

Cristen nodded slowly. "You're right. And that's where we come in."

The next morning, while Billy focused on calibrating the Node fragment, Cristen gathered everyone around a crude diagram she'd sketched on a flattened piece of scrap metal.

"We've been approaching this all wrong," she announced. "Billy can't just be a better pilot—we need a better strategy."

Relson crossed his arms. "What'd you have in mind?"

"Pattern recognition." Cristen tapped the diagram, which showed a series of combat scenarios. "I've been studying footage of Zoltar's tournaments. His champions all have signature moves, predictable attack patterns."

She turned to Billy. "You're thinking like an engineer—looking for the perfect solution. But there isn't one. What we need is adaptability."

"That's where I come in," Relson added, stepping forward with a modified sensor array. "Been working on this all night. It's a predictive defense system—analyzes opponent movements and anticipates strikes before they happen."

Billy examined the device with growing excitement. "This could work. If we integrate it with the Reckoner's neural interface..."

"Exactly." Cristen smiled. "I'll program response patterns based on my observations. Relson's sensors will identify threats. And you, Billy, you'll be free to focus on offensive maneuvers."

"A team," Billy realized, glancing between his friends. "Not just me piloting, but all of us fighting together."

Over the next days, they refined their approach. Cristen spent hours programming combat scenarios, forcing

Billy to react to unexpected attacks. Relson improved the sensor array, testing its sensitivity against increasingly complex threats.

"Don't just dodge!" Cristen called as Billy piloted a partially assembled Reckoner arm against Relson's simulated attacks. "Recognize the pattern, then exploit it!"

Slowly, the strategy evolved. Billy learned to trust the defensive systems, allowing his instincts to guide offensive strikes. Relson's sensors became more sophisticated, capable of detecting subtle shifts in an opponent's weight distribution.

"This might actually work," Juno admitted, watching their progress with grudging approval.

Days blended into nights as they transformed the Reckoner from blueprint to reality. Billy worked tirelessly on the power distribution system, his fingers dancing across circuits as he integrated the Node fragment into the core. The golden shard pulsed with energy, bathing the cave in ethereal light whenever he tested the connections.

"More torque in the left actuator," Billy called out, his voice echoing through the cavern. He slid out from beneath the chassis, face smeared with grease. "The balance is still off."

Relson hefted a salvaged hydraulic piston onto his shoulder. "Got just the thing. Military-grade. Found it buried under a combat mech from last year's tournament."

Cristen worked on programming the neural interface, her eyes reflecting the glow of holographic code projected by Zippy. "Predictive response algorithms at ninety-three percent efficiency," she announced, swiping through data screens. "Still needs fine-tuning for complex attack patterns."

Juno supervised with critical eyes, occasionally offering guidance drawn from years in the arena. "Lower the center of gravity," he advised as they assembled the leg units. "Speed beats strength when you're fighting for survival."

Each morning began with combat drills—Billy learning to anticipate attacks without thinking, to feel the rhythm of battle. Afternoons were devoted to engineering, the four of them working in synchronized harmony as the Reckoner took shape.

"Try it now," Cristen said on the seventh day, stepping back from the neural interface helmet.

Billy slipped it on, closed his eyes, and concentrated. The Reckoner's massive arm rose smoothly, mirroring his own movement with perfect precision.

"It's... responding to my thoughts," he whispered, amazed at how natural it felt.

Relson circled the robot, inspecting the armor plating he'd painstakingly reinforced. "Outer shell can take a direct hit from a plasma cannon now."

Zippy buzzed excitedly around the Reckoner's head, projecting diagnostic readouts that showed all systems functioning at optimal levels.

On the tenth day, they stepped back to behold their creation. The Reckoner stood eighteen feet tall, its frame sleek yet formidable. The Node fragment glowed at its core, pulsing like a mechanical heart.

"It's finished," Billy said, voice filled with wonder and determination. He placed his hand on the cool metal of the robot's leg, feeling the potential humming beneath his fingers.

CHAPTER 11: BONDS FORGED IN FIRE

"Ready for the first live test?" Cristen called from her position at the makeshift control station. Zippy hovered beside her, projecting system diagnostics in the air.

"As ready as we'll ever be." Billy secured the neural interface helmet and climbed into the pilot's cradle. The Golden Node fragment pulsed brighter as he settled into position, its energy responding to his proximity.

Relson gave him a thumbs-up from the ground. "Remember, just basic movements today. No fancy stuff."

Juno stood back, arms crossed, his expression unreadable. "Power levels at thirty percent for the test. No higher."

Billy took a deep breath and closed his eyes. The neural link activated with a soft hum, connecting his mind to the Reckoner's systems. He felt the robot become an extension of himself—massive yet responsive, powerful yet precise.

"Initiating startup sequence," he announced.

The Reckoner's eyes illuminated, casting twin beams of blue light across the cavern. Its servos whirred to life, joints flexing as power flowed through its frame.

"All systems nominal," Cristen confirmed, monitoring the readouts. "Power distribution stable."

Billy focused, willing the machine to move. The

Reckoner's right arm rose smoothly, fingers unfurling in perfect synchronization with Billy's thoughts.

"It works!" Relson shouted, pumping his fist in the air.

"Left leg forward," Billy commanded through the neural link. The massive robot shifted its weight, the floor trembling as it took its first step.

"Power levels holding steady," Cristen reported. "Thirty-two percent and—"

The Golden Node suddenly flared, its light intensifying from gold to blinding white. The Reckoner jerked violently, its movements no longer matching Billy's commands.

"What's happening?" Billy gasped, feeling the neural connection distort. Pain lanced through his temples as conflicting signals flooded the interface.

"Power surge!" Cristen shouted, frantically working the controls. "The Node's output just tripled!"

The Reckoner's arm swung wildly, smashing into a support column. Rocks cascaded from the ceiling as the robot staggered sideways, its movements erratic and dangerous.

"Shut it down!" Juno yelled, pulling Relson away from falling debris.

Billy fought to regain control, but the neural link burned in his mind like fire. "I can't! It's not responding!"

The Reckoner's chest plate split open as the Node's energy overloaded its containment systems. Golden light erupted outward, shorting out the cavern's lighting and plunging them into darkness punctuated only by electrical discharges crackling across the robot's frame.

"Emergency disconnect!" Cristen cried, slamming her hand on the failsafe.

The neural link severed abruptly. Billy slumped in the

pilot's cradle as the Reckoner froze mid-motion, then collapsed to its knees with a thunderous impact that shook the entire cave.

Silence filled the cavern as emergency lights flickered on, casting eerie shadows across the fallen Reckoner. Billy tore off the neural interface helmet and hurled it against the control panel.

"I had it under control!" he shouted, climbing down from the pilot's cradle with shaking hands. "Who touched the power settings?"

Cristen stepped forward, data pad in hand. "Nobody did, Billy. The Node just—"

"You were supposed to monitor the power levels!" Billy's voice echoed through the cavern as he stormed toward her. "Thirty percent, Juno said. Thirty! Not whatever the hell that was!"

Relson moved between them. "Hey, take it easy. We're all figuring this out together."

"Together?" Billy shoved past him, eyes wild. "I'm the one with my brain wired into that thing! I'm the one who felt it trying to tear my mind apart!"

Juno approached cautiously. "The Node is unpredictable. That's why I warned—"

"Your warnings were useless!" Billy spun toward him, jabbing a finger at the older man's chest. "If you knew so much, why didn't you tell me it could surge like that? Or did you forget that detail during your years hiding in a cave?"

Zippy chirped anxiously, hovering near Billy's shoulder, but he swatted the drone away.

"And you!" Billy rounded on Relson. "All those parts you've been bringing in—half of them are junk! The power coupling nearly melted because of that second-rate conductor you salvaged!"

Relson's face hardened. "I've been risking my neck in that scrapyard for weeks while you play mad scientist."

"Maybe if you'd actually paid attention when I explained what we needed instead of—"

"That's enough!" Cristen's voice cut through his tirade. "This isn't helping anything."

"What would you know about it?" Billy snapped, turning his fury toward her. "You can't even understand basic engineering principles! I have to explain everything three times before you—"

"We're trying to help you find your father," Cristen said quietly. "Remember?"

The words hung in the air like a physical blow. Billy's anger faltered, his shoulders slumping as the adrenaline drained away. He looked around at the faces of his friends —hurt, disappointment, and concern reflected back at him.

"I..." He trailed off, unable to form words through the tightness in his throat.

Juno stepped forward, his weathered face solemn. "The Node isn't like other power sources, Billy. It responds to the user's emotions, amplifies them. Your frustration, your fear, your desperation to succeed—it all fed back into the system."

Billy stared at the fallen Reckoner, its frame still crackling with residual energy. "So this is my fault?"

"It's nobody's fault," Cristen said. "But you can't pilot this thing alone. The emotional feedback is too strong."

"I don't need help piloting," Billy insisted, though his voice lacked conviction. "I just need better components, better safeguards."

Relson folded his arms in dismay. "There it is again.

Always the machines that need fixing, never anything else."

"What's that supposed to mean?"

"It means you don't trust us," Relson said bluntly. "Not really. You want our help gathering parts, you want us to follow your instructions, but you don't actually want partners."

Billy opened his mouth to argue, then closed it again. The truth of Relson's words stung worse than any insult.

Zippy hovered nearby, projecting a holographic replay of Billy's outburst. The drone chirped sadly, the sound echoing in the sudden silence.

"I can't afford to fail," Billy finally said, his voice barely above a whisper. "My father's counting on me."

Cristen approached him, careful not to touch the still-smoking neural interface. "Your father worked with a partner, Billy. He and Juno built these machines together. Neither one tried to do it all alone."

Billy looked at Juno, who nodded confirmation.

"I've spent my whole life taking things apart and putting them back together," Billy said. "Machines make sense. They do what you tell them to. People..."

"People surprise you," Juno finished. "They have their own ideas, their own ways of doing things. And sometimes, their way works better than yours."

Repairs took three days. Billy worked methodically, replacing damaged components and recalibrating the neural interface. He still directed most of the work, but something had changed. When Relson suggested a different power routing configuration, Billy actually listened. When Cristen proposed modifications to the control algorithms, he incorporated her ideas without argument.

"Power coupling's fixed," Billy announced, wiping grease from his hands. "Should handle the Node's output more efficiently now."

Juno examined their work with critical eyes. "You've added redundant systems. Smart."

"Cristen's idea," Billy admitted. "She said we needed backups for the backups."

Cristen looked up from her station, surprised by the acknowledgment. "Ready for another test when you are."

Billy hesitated, then tossed her a neural interface headset. "Here. You're piloting with me this time."

"What?" Cristen caught the headset reflexively. "But I've never—"

"The Node responds to emotions," Billy explained. "Mine are too... intense. Too focused on finding my father. But you—" he gestured vaguely, "—you're steadier."

Relson snorted. "That's Billy-speak for 'I need help.'"

"Don't push it," Billy warned, but there was no real heat in his voice.

They climbed into the dual pilot's cradle, adjusting the neural interfaces. Zippy hovered nearby, monitoring their vital signs.

"Power at twenty percent," Juno called out. "Let's be cautious."

Billy nodded. "Initiating neural handshake."

The connection formed—not just between pilots and machine, but between Billy and Cristen themselves. For a moment, Billy felt disoriented as Cristen's consciousness brushed against his own.

"Whoa," Cristen whispered. "Is it supposed to feel like this?"

"Just breathe," Billy instructed. "Let the connection stabilize."

The Reckoner hummed to life, its systems responding to their combined commands. Billy felt the difference immediately—where his thoughts were precise and technical, Cristen's were fluid and intuitive. Together, they created a balance.

"Left arm," Billy directed.

The massive limb rose smoothly.

"Your turn," he told Cristen.

She concentrated, and the right arm mirrored the movement with perfect synchronization.

"Power holding steady at twenty-two percent," Relson reported. "Looking good!"

The test bots emerged from recessed chambers in the cavern wall—three automated combat units Juno had salvaged and reprogrammed for training. Their chassis gleamed dully in the low light, optical sensors tracking the Reckoner's movements.

"Test sequence initiated," Juno announced. "These units are programmed with basic combat routines. Nothing fancy, but they'll coordinate their attacks."

The first bot lunged forward, extending a hydraulic battering ram aimed at the Reckoner's midsection.

"Incoming!" Cristen called through the neural link.

Billy's instinct was to counterattack with brute force, but he felt Cristen's more measured response through their connection. Instead of the hammer blow he'd planned, the Reckoner pivoted sideways, letting the attacker's momentum carry it past.

"Nice dodge," Billy admitted.

"Two more, three o'clock," Cristen warned as the remaining bots circled to flank them.

Billy directed power to the Reckoner's right arm, transforming the hand into a defensive shield just as one bot launched a volley of training projectiles. The impacts rattled against the shield but caused no damage.

Through their neural link, Billy sensed Cristen's idea forming. Without words, he adjusted, allowing her to direct their next move.

The Reckoner dropped to one knee, sweeping its leg in a wide arc that caught the third bot mid-charge. The machine tumbled, circuits sparking.

"Twenty-eight percent power," Relson reported. "Still stable!"

The first bot recovered and rejoined the attack, both remaining units converging simultaneously. Billy felt a spike of anxiety—his old instinct to handle everything himself surging through the neural link.

Cristen's calm flowed back to him. "Together," she said simply.

They moved as one, the Reckoner leaping with surprising grace for its size. It landed behind the bots, catching one in each massive hand before slamming them together with calculated force—enough to disable but not destroy. The test bots powered down, their lights fading to dormancy.

"Combat simulation complete," Juno announced, unable to keep the pride from his voice. "All objectives achieved."

Billy and Cristen disengaged the neural link, both breathing hard but grinning.

"That was..." Billy searched for words.

"Better than doing it alone?" Cristen suggested.

Billy nodded, offering her a hand as they climbed down from the pilot's cradle. "Way better."

Relson clapped Billy on the back. "That was incredible! The way you two moved that thing—it was like watching a dance."

"A really big, dangerous dance," Cristen added, massaging her temples. The neural link left a lingering buzz in her mind.

Juno approached, examining the readouts on his tablet. "Power efficiency is up forty percent from our first test. The dual-pilot system distributes the Node's energy more evenly." He looked up at Billy. "Your father would be impressed."

Billy felt a warmth spread through his chest at the words. "We still need to test the weapons systems and the enhanced mobility protocols."

"Tomorrow," Juno said firmly. "Neural linking is exhausting, especially the first few times. You both need rest."

As if on cue, Zippy chirped and displayed a holographic calendar. The tournament registration deadline flashed in red—just two days away.

"We're cutting it close," Cristen observed.

"But we're ready," Billy said with newfound confidence. "Or we will be."

Later that evening, they gathered around a small fire near the cave entrance. The night air carried a metallic chill, and stars winked through gaps in the scrapyard piles above.

"So what happens after we register?" Relson asked, poking the fire with a metal rod. "Do we get to see the arena? Study the competition?"

Juno shook his head. "Zoltar keeps everything tightly controlled. You'll get a schedule of preliminary matches, but not much else."

Billy stared into the flames. "We still don't know exactly where they're keeping my father."

"The prisoners are usually held in the lower levels," Juno

said quietly. "Beneath the main arena floor."

"Then that's where we'll go after we win," Billy stated.

"*If* we win," Cristen corrected gently.

Billy looked around at his friends—Cristen with her quiet determination, Relson pretending not to be worried, Juno's weathered face showing both hope and fear. Even Zippy hovered closer, as if listening intently.

"No," Billy said with quiet certainty. "When we win. Because we're not just fighting for the prize anymore." He reached out, placing his hand palm-down in the center of their circle. "We're fighting for family."

Cristen placed her hand on top of his without hesitation. Relson followed, then Juno, his scarred hand completing the circle.

"For family," they echoed.

The morning light filtered through the skylights of the cave system, casting long shadows across the Reckoner's massive frame. Billy circled the robot, inspecting the modifications they'd made overnight. The weapons systems were operational, the neural interface refined, but something still felt missing.

"It's too... obvious," Billy muttered, tapping his wrench against his palm.

"What do you mean?" Cristen asked, looking up from her diagnostic panel.

"Tournament bots are flashy, intimidating." Billy gestured at the Reckoner. "This looks like exactly what it is—a serious combat machine. Zoltar will spot it as a threat immediately."

Relson, who had been quietly working in a corner of the cave, cleared his throat. "I might have something for that."

Billy turned, skepticism evident on his face. "What kind

of something?"

Relson approached with a small crate. "Street mods. Stuff the rich engineers at the tournament wouldn't think of." He opened the lid, revealing an assortment of components Billy didn't recognize.

"What is all this?" Billy picked up what looked like a modified sensor array.

"Optical camouflage," Relson explained. "Used by smugglers in the Eastern District. Makes your heat signature read differently to thermal scanners."

Billy examined the device with newfound interest. "This would mask our power core from pre-match scans."

"Exactly." Relson pulled out another component. "And this? Acoustic dampener. The big bots all make noise— hydraulics, servos, cooling systems. This absorbs sound waves, makes you quieter in the arena."

"Giving us a stealth advantage," Cristen realized.

Relson nodded, growing more confident. "I also brought black market reaction enhancers for the joint servos. They're technically illegal in professional matches, but they're undetectable if installed right."

Billy stared at Relson, seeing him in a new light. "Where did you learn about all this?"

"You think you're the only one who knows machines?" Relson shrugged, but couldn't hide his pride. "When you grow up having to steal parts to stay alive, you learn which mods actually work and which ones get you caught."

Billy picked up each component, examining them with growing appreciation. "These are brilliant. Why didn't you mention them before?"

"Wasn't sure you'd listen," Relson admitted. "You've got your fancy engineering, and I've got... street tricks."

Billy extended his hand. "Well, I'm listening now. Show me how to install them."

The modifications took hours, but transformed the Reckoner. Where before it had looked formidable but conventional, now it carried an air of dangerous mystery. The optical camouflage shimmered subtly across its surface, distorting its true dimensions. The acoustic dampeners turned its thunderous footsteps into whispers.

The small drone zipped around the Reckoner, scanning every component before projecting a holographic readout. All systems showed green.

"It's ready," Billy announced. "We're ready."

They packed the Reckoner's components into specially designed transport crates—another of Relson's contributions. The modular design allowed them to move the massive machine in pieces without attracting attention.

"Remember," Juno warned as they prepared to leave the cave, "once you register, Zoltar's people will be watching. You can't come back here. It's too risky."

"What about you?" Cristen asked.

Juno shook his head. "I can't show my face at the arena. Zoltar thinks I'm dead, and that's an advantage we need to keep."

"But we'll need your guidance," Billy protested.

Juno handed him a small communication device. "This operates on frequencies the tournament security doesn't monitor. I'll be watching from a distance, advising when I can."

Billy tucked the device into his tool belt. "We'll see you on the other side, then."

"Be careful," Juno said, his weathered face solemn. "Zoltar

doesn't just want to win—he wants to own the winners. Don't let your guard down, even for a moment."

As they loaded the final crate onto their makeshift transport, Billy paused, looking back at the cave that had become their workshop and refuge. "Thank you," he said to Juno. "For everything."

The older man nodded, emotion flickering across his face. "Your father would be proud. Not just of the machine you've built, but of the team you've brought together."

With the Reckoner packed and ready, they set out toward the city center, where Zoltar's towering arena complex dominated the skyline. The tournament registration center would be crowded with last-minute entrants—the perfect cover for their arrival.

"Next stop," Billy said, determination hardening his voice, "the arena."

CHAPTER 12: THE RECKONING RISES

The journey to the arena meant traversing several districts, each more dangerous than the last. Billy punched a sequence into his wrist console, activating the Reckoner's guard protocols. Though packed in transport crates, its sensors remained active, scanning their surroundings.

"Reckoner, guard mode active," Billy confirmed as small indicator lights blinked to life on the largest crate. "Motion detection radius set to twenty meters."

"Will it attack if someone gets too close?" Relson asked, eyeing the crate nervously.

"No, just alerts us," Billy replied. "Can't have it blasting holes through civilians."

They pushed their transport cart through the narrow streets of the Southern District, keeping to the shadows where possible. The weight of their mission hung heavy in the silence between them.

Cristen fell into step beside Billy, studying his face. The determined set of his jaw couldn't hide the anxiety in his eyes.

"So," she began carefully, "we might actually find your father at this tournament. How are you feeling about that?"

Billy kept his eyes forward, focusing on navigating the

cart around a pothole. "I don't know. I've imagined meeting him a thousand different ways."

"And?"

"And now that it might actually happen..." He trailed off, adjusting his welding goggles on his head. "What if he doesn't recognize me? What if he doesn't want to be found?"

Cristen let the question hang between them for a moment. "He left you that message, Billy. He wanted you to find him."

"That was years ago. What if he's different now? What if I'm not what he expected?"

"You mean what if you're not the perfect robot engineer he hoped for?" Cristen smiled. "Because from where I'm standing, you've built something incredible with spare parts and determination."

Billy shook his head. "It's not just that. I've spent my whole life wondering about him, building this image in my head. What if the real person doesn't match?"

"Then you'll get to know the real person," Cristen said simply. "That's how it works with people, Billy. They're not machines with blueprints. You discover them piece by piece."

Billy nodded slowly, considering her words. "I just hope he's still alive."

The conversation died as they approached the edge of the industrial district. Billy's hand instinctively moved to his tool belt, sensing something off about the stillness ahead. "Guys..." Relson whispered, pointing upward.

Three sleek black drones hovered silently above the adjacent rooftops, their red sensor arrays tracking the group's movement. Each bore Zoltar's insignia—a stylized Z surrounded by lightning bolts.

"Keep moving," Billy muttered. "Act normal."

They hadn't gone twenty paces when the drones descended in perfect formation, blocking their path. A fourth and fifth appeared from behind, boxing them in.

"Scanner detect contraband tech," came a robotic voice from the lead drone. "Surrender cargo for inspection."

Billy's hand closed around a small device on his belt. "Not happening."

The drones' weapon ports snapped open simultaneously. "Final warning. Surrender cargo or—"

Relson hurled a piece of scrap metal at the nearest drone, striking its sensor array. "Run!"

The drones attacked with precision, firing stun pulses that scorched the pavement around them. Billy dove behind the cart, pulling Cristen down with him. Relson rolled beneath a nearby dumpster.

"Zippy, defensive maneuvers!" Billy shouted.

The little scout bot shot from Billy's backpack, chirping frantically as it zipped between the attacking drones, confusing their targeting systems.

Cristen pulled her tech bow from her back, nocking an electromagnetic disruptor arrow. "I need a clear shot!"

A stun pulse grazed Billy's shoulder, sending numbing pain down his arm. He gritted his teeth, fumbling with his tool belt to activate a portable shield generator.

"Billy, they're trying to steal the Reckoner!" Relson shouted, pointing to two drones attempting to lift the main cargo crate.

Then, without warning, one of the drones simply exploded in midair. The others paused, sensors whirring in confusion. Seconds later, a second drone detonated, followed by a third.

The remaining drones backed away, their flight patterns

suddenly erratic. Then they too exploded in quick succession, raining smoking parts onto the street.

Silence fell. Billy, Cristen, and Relson exchanged bewildered looks.

"What just happened?" Cristen whispered, lowering her bow.

Billy approached the smoldering remains of the nearest drone, kneeling to examine the circuitry. "I... I don't know. They just... failed catastrophically."

"Did you do something?" Relson asked, emerging from his hiding spot.

Billy shook his head. "No. Nothing. They just... exploded."

Zippy circled the wreckage, scanning and beeping in confusion.

"This doesn't make sense," Billy muttered, turning a scorched circuit board over in his hands. "Something caused a cascade failure in their power cores, but I can't see what triggered it."

Billy turned the scorched circuit board over, his fingers tracing the intricate pathways that no scrap yard tech could match. The drone components were unlike anything he'd ever seen—miniaturized quantum processors, self-repairing nanomesh, power cells that shouldn't exist outside theoretical papers.

"This is... impossible," he whispered, holding up a tiny component for the others to see. "This circuitry is years beyond anything available to the public."

Cristen leaned in, her eyes widening. "Is that a neural integration chip? Those are illegal everywhere."

"Not just illegal—they're supposed to be impossible to manufacture," Billy replied, his voice tight with worry. "These drones weren't just surveillance. They were capable of making autonomous kill decisions."

Relson kicked at another piece of wreckage. "So what does that mean for us?"

"It means we're up against someone with resources beyond what we imagined." Billy pocketed the component, his hands trembling slightly. "If these are just his perimeter drones, what kind of tech does Zoltar have inside that arena?"

They fell silent, the implications sinking in. The Reckoner, their pride and achievement, suddenly seemed primitive by comparison.

"We should move," Cristen finally said, scanning the rooftops nervously. "More might come."

They pushed onward through the industrial district, the transport cart's wheels clattering against the broken pavement. Every shadow seemed to hide potential threats, every distant hum a possible drone squadron.

"My father knew," Billy said suddenly. "That's why he disappeared instead of confronting Zoltar directly. He knew what we were really up against."

Zippy chirped anxiously from Billy's shoulder, its sensors continually scanning their surroundings.

"You think your dad sabotaged those drones somehow?" Relson asked.

Billy shook his head. "I don't know. But someone did."

As they approached the outskirts of the tournament district, the sprawling arena came into view—a massive structure of gleaming metal and pulsing lights, surrounded by security barriers and patrolling guards. Propaganda videos played on enormous screens, showing highlights from previous tournaments and glamorized images of Zoltar himself.

"Look at him," Cristen whispered, pointing to a close-up of Zoltar's face on one of the screens. "He's not even trying to hide it anymore."

The camera lingered on Zoltar's eyes—cold, calculating, utterly devoid of empathy as he watched combatants tear each other apart for his amusement.

"He's not just running a tournament," Billy realized. "He's harvesting technology and engineers. And he's been doing it for years."

The registration booth stood at the edge of the arena complex—a stark contrast to the gleaming tournament facilities beyond. Three bored officials processed the line of hopeful contestants, most of whom looked like they'd cobbled together fighting machines from whatever scrap they could find.

"Remember," Billy whispered as they approached the front of the line, "we're just another underdog team. Nothing special.'

Cristen nodded, keeping her tech bow concealed beneath her jacket. "Zippy should stay hidden until we're in our pit."

"Next!" barked a woman with cybernetic implants running along her jawline. Her eyes flicked between them suspiciously. "Team name?"

"Bolts Brigade," Billy replied, sliding their hastily forged credentials across the counter.

The woman scanned the documents with a handheld device, her expression unchanging. "Contestant profile?"

"Class three combat chassis with modified hydraulics," Billy recited the rehearsed description, deliberately understating the Reckoner's capabilities. "Nothing fancy."

Her implants pulsed with blue light as she accessed their information. "First-time contestants. Pit assignment 42, east quadrant." She handed them security badges. "These give you access to your pit and common areas only.

Restricted zones will trigger security response. Clear?"

"Crystal," Billy replied, accepting the badges.

"Inspection team will verify your bot meets regulation standards before your first match tomorrow at 0900. Any illegal modifications will result in immediate disqualification." She glanced at their transport cart. "Those crates look heavy for amateurs."

Relson stepped forward with a casual shrug. "We believe in overbuilding. Better too much material than not enough, right?"

The woman's eyes narrowed, but she waved them through. "Next!"

They wheeled their cargo through security scanners that Billy had specifically shielded their equipment against. Guards with neural-linked weapons watched them pass, their eyes cold and evaluating.

Pit 42 was smaller than Billy had hoped—a cramped maintenance bay with oil-stained floors and flickering lights. The walls were thin enough that they could hear other teams working in adjacent pits, the sounds of welding and hydraulic testing creating a constant mechanical symphony.

"Home sweet home," Relson muttered, securing the door behind them.

Billy immediately activated a signal jammer from his tool belt. "Zippy, scan for surveillance."

The little drone emerged from Billy's backpack, circling the room while emitting soft chirps. After a thorough sweep, Zippy projected a holographic map showing three hidden cameras and a microphone embedded in the ceiling.

"Amateur hour," Billy whispered, pointing to the surveillance devices. "Let's give them a show."

Cristen and Relson put on a performance of mundane preparation—unpacking basic tools and arranging them conspicuously while Billy used Zippy to create localized electromagnetic interference around each surveillance device. To any observer, they appeared to be just another amateur team setting up shop.

"Now we can talk," Billy whispered once the jammers were in place. "But keep it casual. Body language can give us away even if they can't hear us."

They began unpacking the Reckoner, piece by carefully engineered piece. What looked like scrap metal to untrained eyes was in fact revolutionary robotics disguised beneath a veneer of rust and dents.

"Registration seemed too easy," Cristen murmured, pretending to inspect a joint connector. "I expected more scrutiny."

"They want us here," Billy replied, assembling what appeared to be a standard hydraulic piston but was actually part of the Reckoner's advanced propulsion system. "The more contestants, the better the show."

Relson peered through a gap in the bay door. "Lots of security for a sporting event. Those guards aren't just watching for troublemakers—they're scanning faces."

"Looking for someone specific?" Cristen asked.

Billy's hands stilled momentarily. "Or looking for my father. If he escaped, they might think he'd try to make contact during the tournament."

Zippy chirped quietly from inside an empty crate, projecting a small hologram showing a map of the facility. The little drone had already begun mapping escape routes and identifying security protocols.

"We should split up," Billy suggested. "Relson, see what you can learn from the other teams. Cristen, try to get a feel for the arena layout. I'll finish assembly here."

"What about your father?" Cristen asked. "Where do we even start looking?"

Billy pulled a small device from his tool belt—the frequency scanner Juno had given them. "If he's here, he'll be communicating somehow. This might help us find him."

"And if Zoltar spots us first?" Relson asked.

Billy's expression hardened as he connected the Reckoner's neural interface. "Then we give him exactly what he wants—a show he'll never forget."

As they worked into the evening, the Reckoner's frame took shape beneath their hands. Billy connected neural pathways while Cristen calibrated the targeting systems. Relson had returned with valuable intel about their first opponent—a hulking crusher-type bot with predictable attack patterns but devastating power.

A soft knock at their pit door froze them all in place.

"Security inspection," came a muffled voice.

Billy nodded to Relson, who positioned himself to block the view of their more advanced components while Cristen casually draped a tarp over the Reckoner's neural core.

"Coming," Billy called, preparing to open the bay door.

He cracked the door open, expecting to see the stern face of a tournament official. Instead, he found himself staring at a clean-cut man in pressed maintenance coveralls. The stranger wore thick-rimmed glasses and had slicked-back hair beneath a standard-issue tournament cap. His clean-shaven face looked oddly naked, like someone had stripped away a natural part of him.

Billy's hand tightened on the door. Something about

the man's posture was familiar—the slight hunch of shoulders more accustomed to ducking through low passages.

"Routine systems check," the man said, holding up a clipboard. His voice was pitched higher than normal, but Billy caught the undertone of gravel beneath the forced lightness.

The man's eyes met Billy's, and in that moment, recognition clicked.

"Caveman?" Billy whispered, barely audible.

The man gave an almost imperceptible nod before saying loudly, "Just need to verify your power hookups are up to code."

Billy stepped back, allowing him to enter. Once inside, Juno—the Caveman—maintained his act, moving to the power junction and pretending to take readings.

"What are you doing here?" Cristen hissed when the door closed. "And what happened to your—" she gestured to his face and clothes.

"Couldn't let you kids face this alone," Juno muttered, still pretending to check wiring. "Figured I'd be more use without looking like I crawled out of a trash compactor."

"How did you even get in?" Relson asked.

Juno tapped his maintenance badge. "You'd be surprised what people don't question when you look like you belong."

Juno moved methodically around the pit, maintaining his cover while speaking in hushed tones. "Tournament security's tighter than I've ever seen it. They've got neural-linked guards at every access point and quantum scanners checking every component that enters the arena."

"How did you know where to find us?" Billy asked,

pretending to help with the inspection.

"Followed the explosions," Juno replied with a slight smile. "Those drones that attacked you? They've been hunting for anything unusual entering the tournament zone. You're lucky I was nearby."

Billy's eyes widened. "That was you? How did you—"

"Let's just say I learned a few tricks during my time as champion." Juno pulled a small device from his pocket. "Electromagnetic pulse emitter. Designed it myself years ago. Zoltar's tech has gotten more advanced, but the basic vulnerabilities remain the same."

Cristen moved closer. "Have you seen any sign of Billy's father?"

Juno's expression darkened. "No. But I've found something else." He lowered his voice further. "There's a restricted section beneath the main arena. Heavily guarded, no maintenance access. Whatever Zoltar's really doing here, that's where you'll find answers."

"How do we get in?" Relson asked.

"You don't—not directly." Juno pulled out a small circuit board from his toolkit. "But this might help. It's a bypass module for the arena's neural interface. When you connect to battle, it'll give you limited access to the facility's systems."

Billy examined the circuit. "This could work, but it's risky. If they detect the intrusion—"

"They'll shut you down before you can blink," Juno finished. "That's why timing is everything. You'll only get one shot."

Zippy chirped quietly from inside the crate, projecting a small hologram of the arena's layout with the restricted area highlighted.

"Your little friend's already mapping the system," Juno

observed with approval. "Smart."

"Tomorrow's our first match," Billy said. "If we win convincingly enough, we might get Zoltar's attention."

"That's what I'm afraid of," Juno replied grimly. "Be careful what you wish for."

CHAPTER 13: CLASH OF TITANS

Juno glanced at his watch and cursed under his breath. "I need to go. Guards rotate every twenty minutes."

After he left, Billy slumped into the pilot's chair, turning the bypass module over in his hands. The weight of their mission pressed down on him like the tons of metal surrounding them in the arena.

"We need to focus on winning our first match," Relson said, pulling up the schematics of their opponent. "That crusher bot won't know what hit it."

Cristen studied Billy's face. "You're thinking about something else, aren't you?"

Billy nodded slowly. "I came here to find my father, but..."

"But what?" Relson asked.

"The Reckoner could actually win this thing." Billy's eyes lit up as he ran his hand along the control panel. "With the modifications we've made, the Golden Node power source, Juno's training—we could go all the way."

"Isn't that the plan?" Relson asked. "Win the tournament, get face time with Zoltar, find your dad?"

Billy shook his head. "If we use Juno's bypass module during our first match, we might be able to locate my father immediately. But it would mean risking disqualification—or worse."

"Or," Cristen said, understanding dawning on her

face, "we play it straight, advance through the ranks legitimately, and become the champions everyone's watching."

"Glory versus rescue," Billy muttered. "If we win it all, we'd have the spotlight, the resources, maybe even enough influence to force Zoltar's hand publicly."

Zippy chirped anxiously, projecting two different paths on the floor—one leading to a restricted area, the other to the championship podium.

"What would your father want you to do?" Cristen asked softly.

Billy stared at the projection, the two paths diverging before him like roads in a forest. The safe path of glory and public acclaim, or the dangerous road of immediate rescue with all its risks.

"I don't know," he admitted. "I barely know him."

Billy's fingers tightened around the bypass module. Outside their pit area, the crowd's roar swelled as the previous match concluded. They had minutes before their first-round battle.

"My father disappeared trying to expose Zoltar." Billy stood up, decision crystallizing in his mind. "If I choose glory over finding him, I'm no better than the people who forgot him."

Relson frowned. "But if we get caught—"

"We'll be caught anyway if we win enough matches," Billy said. "Zoltar will recognize The Reckoner's design eventually. It's based on my father's blueprints."

Cristen placed her hand on Billy's shoulder. "You're sure about this?"

"For thirteen years I've wondered where he is, what happened to him." Billy's voice cracked slightly. "I can't wait any longer."

He slid the bypass module into his pocket and climbed up to The Reckoner's cockpit. Zippy followed, beeping encouragement.

"Here's the plan," Billy said as the others joined him. "We fight legitimately, but I'll route Zippy through the arena's systems during the match. The bypass module will let him access restricted areas of Zoltar's network while everyone's distracted by our fight."

Cristen nodded. "The perfect cover."

"If Zippy finds anything about your dad?" Relson asked.

Billy's jaw set firmly. "Then we make our move immediately. Tournament be damned."

The warning klaxon sounded. Five minutes to their match.

"What if..." Relson hesitated. "What if your dad isn't even here anymore?"

The question hung in the air. Billy had avoided considering this possibility for weeks.

"Then at least I'll know," he said finally. "And we can focus on winning and taking Zoltar down properly."

He inserted Zippy's uplink cable into the console. The little drone chirped excitedly, its eyes flashing as it prepared for its mission.

"Ready?" Billy asked his friends.

Cristen took her position at the weapons console. "For your father."

Relson grabbed the auxiliary controls. "Let's make some noise."

Billy powered up the Golden Node, feeling its energy pulse through the machine. "For my father," he whispered, "and for the truth."

The arena doors began their slow ascent, revealing the cavernous battleground beyond. Blinding spotlights swept across The Reckoner's frame, drawing thunderous applause from the packed stands. Billy's hands trembled slightly on the controls.

A sharp knock on the cockpit hatch startled him. Juno's face appeared at the small window, his expression urgent. Billy cracked the hatch open.

"You've got ninety seconds before they lock this thing down for combat," Juno said, his voice low and intense. "Listen to me, kid."

Billy nodded, suddenly aware of how dry his mouth had become.

"I've watched you train. I've seen you overthink every move, second-guess every decision." Juno's eyes bored into Billy's. "That ends now. In there, hesitation gets you scrapped."

"But what if—"

Juno cut him off with a sharp gesture. "No 'what ifs.' Commit one hundred percent and let yourself trust your training. No second guesses!"

Billy swallowed hard. "But the bypass module, finding my father—"

"Same principle," Juno said firmly. "You made your plan. Now execute it with complete conviction. Half-measures get you nowhere in the arena or in life." He glanced at the countdown timer. "Your father would tell you the same thing."

"How do you know?" Billy asked.

A ghost of a smile crossed Juno's face. "Because I knew him. Melvin never did anything halfway. Neither should his son."

The final warning klaxon sounded. Juno stepped back.

"Commit fully, Billy. To the fight, to your friends, to finding your father. No looking back."

As the hatch sealed shut, Billy felt a strange calm settle over him. Zippy chirped encouragingly from the console where he was plugged in, ready to infiltrate Zoltar's systems.

"You heard the man," Billy said to Cristen and Relson. "No second guesses."

He grasped the controls with newfound steadiness as The Reckoner lurched forward into the blinding lights of the arena.

The crowd's roar hit them like a physical force as The Reckoner stepped into the arena. Thirty feet of imposing metal and salvaged parts, moving with surprising grace under Billy's control. The massive combat bot cast long shadows across the sand-covered floor under the harsh spotlights.

"Ladies and gentlemen!" The announcer's voice boomed through speakers that shook the very foundations. "Our next challenger is a true unknown! Coming from the Southern District scrapyards, I give you... THE RECKONER!"

The audience erupted, their cheers echoing throughout the cavernous space. Billy felt the vibrations through the control sticks in his hands.

"They love us," Relson whispered, awe in his voice. "They actually love us."

Cristen monitored the weapons systems. "They love an underdog. Don't let it distract you."

Billy nodded, keeping his focus as the spotlight followed their machine's slow procession toward the center of the arena. Giant screens overhead displayed The Reckoner from multiple angles, highlighting the patchwork armor that concealed cutting-edge technology beneath.

Zippy chirped softly as it began its infiltration of the

arena's systems, the bypass module glowing faintly beneath the console. No one watching would notice the little drone's secondary mission.

"And facing our newcomers," the announcer continued, "the undefeated crusher of the East Quadrant preliminary rounds... STEEL BEHEMOTH!"

From the opposite entrance, a gleaming black and chrome machine rolled forward on massive treads, its hydraulic arms ending in serrated pincers that snapped menacingly at the air.

Billy took a deep breath, settling into the pilot's seat as The Reckoner reached its starting position. He felt strangely calm now, Juno's words echoing in his mind. No second guesses. Commit fully.

The crowd's noise faded to a distant hum as Billy centered himself. This was it. No turning back. Whatever came next—finding his father, winning the tournament, confronting Zoltar—it all started here, in this moment.

The Reckoner stood tall, its mismatched frame illuminated by spotlights, waiting for the signal to begin.

As Steel Behemoth advanced, time seemed to slow for Billy. His hands moved automatically across the controls, but his mind drifted to memories long buried.

His mother's face appeared before him—not as she was now, but as she had been when he was five, kneeling beside him as he dismantled the kitchen chronometer. Her eyes had flashed with momentary anger, then softened into something else entirely.

"You're just like your father," she'd whispered, helping him gather the tiny gears.

Billy remembered the night she'd worked double shifts at the recycling plant for three months straight to buy him his first tool set. How her hands had been raw and cracked from sorting through chemical waste, yet still gentle as she presented him with the gift.

"I don't understand half of what you build," she'd told him on his tenth birthday, after he'd constructed a miniature water purifier for their apartment. "But I know it matters."

The memory shifted to her sitting alone at their kitchen table, bills spread before her, head in her hands when she thought he was asleep. The sacrifices she never spoke about—the promotion she'd declined because it would have meant moving away from the scrapyard that fed his inventions, the dates she'd canceled to help him search for rare parts.

He remembered her patience when he'd accidentally short-circuited their entire apartment block. Instead of punishment, she'd helped him understand what went wrong, staying up all night as he fixed the damage.

"It's okay to make mistakes," she'd said. "It's not okay to stop trying."

Even when his obsession with robots had intensified after discovering his father's message, she hadn't tried to dissuade him. Instead, she'd opened the sealed workshop, knowing what it would mean—that he would follow this path wherever it led.

"You have his brilliance," she'd told him, "but you have my heart. Don't lose either one."

Steel Behemoth was twenty feet away now, pincers raised for its first attack. Billy blinked away the memories, feeling a new resolve course through him.

Everything—his mother's love, his father's legacy, his own journey—had led him to this moment.

CHAPTER 14: DECEPTIONS IN STEAM

Steel Behemoth lunged forward, its massive pincers snapping toward The Reckoner's midsection. Billy's fingers flew across the controls, muscle memory taking over.

"Cristen, power to the legs!"

The Reckoner pivoted with unexpected agility, the enemy's pincers closing on empty air. Billy felt the machine respond to his commands like an extension of his own body.

"Relson, we need that shield!"

"On it!" Relson slammed a sequence of buttons, deploying the makeshift shield they'd crafted from scrapyard plating.

Steel Behemoth's second attack hit the shield with a thunderous crash that reverberated through the arena. The impact sent The Reckoner sliding backward, leaving deep grooves in the sand.

"Left arm stabilizers failing," Cristen called out, her voice steady despite the danger. "Rerouting power."

Billy nodded, already compensating by shifting the robot's weight. "We can't take another hit like that."

Steel Behemoth's operators sensed weakness and pressed their advantage, the machine charging forward on grinding treads.

"They're trying to pin us against the wall," Billy muttered. "Not happening."

He yanked both control sticks sideways, sending The Reckoner into a controlled fall that caught their opponent off guard. As they hit the ground, Billy triggered the emergency thrusters they'd salvaged from an old cargo lifter.

The Reckoner skidded beneath Steel Behemoth's reach, sand spraying in all directions. The crowd roared at the unexpected maneuver.

"Now!" Billy shouted.

Cristen activated the electromagnetic pulse they'd modified from Zippy's systems. It wasn't powerful enough to disable their opponent completely, but it scrambled Steel Behemoth's targeting systems just long enough.

The Reckoner sprang back to its feet, servos whining with the effort. Billy drove it forward, closing the distance before Steel Behemoth could recover.

"Hydraulic hammer!" he called.

Relson slammed the activation switch. The Reckoner's right arm transformed, panels sliding back to reveal the massive piston they'd constructed from Caveman's old combat parts.

The hammer struck Steel Behemoth's central processor housing with precision, cracking its protective shell. The enemy robot staggered, its movements becoming erratic.

"One more!" Billy called, sweat dripping down his face as he fought to maintain control of their straining machine.

The Reckoner moved in for the finishing blow when Steel Behemoth's operator triggered their hidden weapon. A massive electrified grappling hook shot from its chest cavity, piercing The Reckoner's shoulder joint. Electricity surged through the connection, overloading circuits throughout Billy's creation.

"Systems failing!" Cristen shouted as warning lights flooded their control panel.

The Reckoner's movements stuttered, then froze completely. Inside the cockpit, displays flickered and died. The acrid smell of burnt circuitry filled the cramped space.

Billy frantically worked the controls. "No, no, no—come on!"

"Primary power's down," Relson reported, his voice tight. "Auxiliary isn't responding either."

Steel Behemoth capitalized on their vulnerability, charging forward and delivering a devastating blow to The Reckoner's midsection. The impact sent shockwaves through the cockpit, throwing all three of them against their restraints. Billy's head slammed against the control panel, stars exploding across his vision.

The crowd's roar seemed distant now, muffled by the ringing in his ears. The Reckoner stood immobilized as Steel Behemoth circled, preparing for another strike.

"Dad wouldn't give up," Billy whispered, tasting blood from his split lip. His fingers found the emergency restart sequence they'd installed—a last resort that would burn out several systems but might give them one final chance.

"Billy, if we do that—" Cristen started.

"We have to." His hand hovered over the sequence. "Trust me."

Relson nodded grimly. "Do it."

Billy punched in the code and slammed his palm against the activation panel. For one terrible moment, nothing happened. Then The Reckoner shuddered back to life, its systems rebooting with a series of mechanical groans.

Steel Behemoth was already mid-charge when The Reckoner's eyes flickered back on. Billy had only seconds to react. He threw all remaining power into the legs and core stabilizers, bracing for impact.

The two machines collided with earth-shaking force. The Reckoner absorbed the blow, circuits screaming in protest, but remained standing. Billy felt something click inside him—a moment of perfect clarity amid the chaos.

"We're still in this fight," he said, his voice steady despite the blood trickling down his forehead. "Let's show them what The Reckoner can do."

Steel Behemoth recovered its balance, servos whining as it reoriented toward The Reckoner. The damaged machine pivoted awkwardly on its treads, pincers extended for another devastating attack.

"They're coming in again!" Cristen called, fingers flying across her control panel.

Billy narrowed his eyes, spotting a vulnerability in the enemy's movement pattern. "I see it. Their left tread's running hot—overcompensating for damage on the right side."

The pincers shot forward in a lightning-fast strike that should have caught The Reckoner square in the chest. Instead, Billy jerked both control sticks sharply left, throwing their machine into a sideways roll that defied its massive size.

The Reckoner dropped low, hydraulics hissing as it slid beneath the attack. The crowd gasped at the unexpected display of agility from such a hulking machine.

"Relson, give me everything we've got in the auxiliary thrusters!"

"Already on it!" Relson slammed a series of switches, redirecting power.

The Reckoner's back thrusters ignited with a roar, propelling them in a tight arc around Steel Behemoth's flank. The enemy robot tried to pivot, but its damaged systems couldn't match The Reckoner's sudden burst of speed.

"Perfect!" Billy's hands danced across the controls. "Now!"

The Reckoner extended its reinforced arm, fingers transforming into razor-sharp claws as they raked across Steel Behemoth's exposed tread assembly. Metal shrieked against metal as The Reckoner's claws dug deep, catching the heavy treads and yanking with mechanical strength.

"Hold on!" Billy shouted as The Reckoner braced its legs and pulled.

The tread separated from Steel Behemoth's wheels with a thunderous snap, sending fragments of metal flying across the arena. The enemy robot lurched violently, its weight suddenly unbalanced, and began to spin helplessly on its remaining tread.

The crowd erupted in wild cheers as Steel Behemoth rotated in place, its operators frantically trying to compensate for the catastrophic damage.

"We've got them!" Relson pumped his fist in the air.

"Don't celebrate yet," Billy cautioned, keeping The Reckoner at a safe distance as their opponent continued to spin. "They're wounded, not beaten."

Steel Behemoth's operators weren't surrendering yet. The damaged robot stabilized its spinning, compensating with emergency braking systems. Its remaining weapons systems came online—panels sliding open across its chassis to reveal an array of projectile launchers.

"Incoming!" Cristen shouted as the first volley of metal spikes erupted from Steel Behemoth.

Billy gripped the controls tighter, feeling The Reckoner

respond to his commands with perfect synchronicity. The massive machine ducked with surprising grace, the projectiles whistling overhead to embed in the arena wall. "They're desperate," Billy muttered. "Time to end this."

He pushed The Reckoner forward, accelerating directly toward their wounded opponent. Steel Behemoth fired another barrage, but Billy was ready. He twisted the controls, sending The Reckoner into a sideways slide that carried them beneath the deadly projectiles.

"Relson, divert all remaining power to the legs!"

"You got it!" Relson slammed the sequence, rerouting energy from non-critical systems.

The Reckoner's leg servos whined as fresh power surged through them. Billy could feel the machine gathering itself like a coiled spring.

Steel Behemoth's operators realized their danger too late. The damaged robot tried to pivot away, its single functioning tread grinding frantically against the arena floor. Its arms flailed wildly, trying to keep The Reckoner at bay.

Billy weaved The Reckoner through the desperate defense, ducking beneath one massive arm and sidestepping another. The crowd's roar built to a deafening crescendo as The Reckoner closed the distance.

"Now!" Billy shouted.

The Reckoner planted its right foot and pivoted, hydraulics hissing as its left leg chambered. For a split second, the thirty-foot machine seemed to hang in perfect balance—then Billy triggered the final attack sequence.

The Reckoner's left leg shot forward with devastating force, striking Steel Behemoth square in the center mass. The impact transferred through the wounded machine with catastrophic effect, buckling armor plating and shattering internal support structures.

Steel Behemoth lifted completely off the ground, its massive form suspended in midair for one impossible moment before crashing down with an earth-shaking impact. It lay motionless, systems flickering and dying as emergency shutdown protocols engaged.

The arena fell silent, then erupted in thunderous applause.

From the observation lounge, Zoltar watched the match through narrowed eyes. His skeletal fingers tightened around the armrest of his hovering chair, knuckles whitening beneath paper-thin skin. The unexpected victory of The Reckoner sent ripples of excitement through the elite spectators surrounding him, but Zoltar remained unnaturally still.

"Impressive recovery," murmured one of his advisors. "The boy shows his father's ingenuity."

Zoltar silenced him with a sharp glance. He leaned forward, mechanical components in his chair whirring softly as he studied The Reckoner's damaged frame. Behind the opulent glass partition, he could see the cockpit opening, with Billy emerging victorious.

"The power distribution during that final sequence," he said quietly. "That wasn't in any of Melvin's designs."

His fingers danced across the holographic display embedded in his chair's arm. Data streams scrolled past, analyzing The Reckoner's performance metrics. Something in the numbers made his mouth twitch into a cold smile.

"The Golden Node," he whispered. "So the rumors were true."

He tapped another command, and security camera

feeds from around the arena appeared. His gaze settled on one particular figure standing in the shadows of the maintenance bay—Juno Kett, cleaned up but unmistakable to someone who'd once known him well.

"The Caveman returns to civilization," Zoltar mused. "How convenient."

The crowd continued to cheer as The Reckoner raised its massive arm in victory. Zoltar's expression remained calculated, almost pleased, as he closed the data feeds with a dismissive gesture.

"Prepare my private laboratory," he instructed the aide hovering nearby. "And double the security detail for the semifinals. I want monitoring drones tracking The Reckoner's every movement."

As the aide hurried away, Zoltar turned back to the arena. Below, Billy Applebaum stood triumphant, his father's welding goggles pushed up on his forehead, revealing eyes alight with determination.

"Like father, like son," Zoltar whispered to himself. "But this time, I'll be ready."

The crowd's roar crescendoed as the arena announcer's voice boomed through the speakers: "Ladies and gentlemen, please welcome our tournament sponsor and visionary founder—Zoltar!"

A hush fell over the spectators as a section of the arena floor slid open. From the darkness below, a platform rose smoothly, bearing Zoltar in his hovering chair. The contraption gleamed with polished chrome and pulsing blue light, supporting his frail form with an intricate framework of mechanical arms and medical apparatus.

"What an extraordinary display of ingenuity!" Zoltar's voice carried effortlessly across the arena, amplified by hidden speakers. His face, projected on massive screens, showed a perfect mask of grandfatherly pride. "This is precisely why we hold the tournament—to discover raw talent and nurture the next generation of brilliant minds!"

Billy stood beside The Reckoner's massive foot, sweat and oil streaking his face. Cristen and Relson flanked him, their expressions a mixture of triumph and wariness.

Zoltar's hover chair glided forward, bringing him closer to the victorious team. The crowd applauded as he extended a bony hand toward Billy.

"Young man, your machine shows... familiar innovation." His smile remained fixed, but his eyes—cold and calculating—locked onto Billy's. "The way you adapted mid-battle reminds me of another competitor from years past."

Billy felt a chill despite the arena's heat. "Thank you, sir. I've studied the greats."

"Indeed." Zoltar's voice dropped slightly, audible only to those standing nearby. "Your father would be proud—if he could see you now."

The crowd continued cheering, oblivious to the exchange. To them, it appeared as a generous sponsor congratulating a promising newcomer. But Billy heard the threat beneath the pleasantries.

Zoltar's mechanical chair hummed as he leaned closer. "I look forward to seeing what other... family techniques you've inherited. The semifinals will be quite illuminating."

Billy straightened his shoulders, meeting Zoltar's gaze directly. He adjusted his father's welding goggles on his forehead—a small gesture that didn't escape Zoltar's notice.

"I'm just getting started," Billy replied, his voice steady

despite the hammering of his heart.

Zoltar's smile tightened almost imperceptibly. "As am I, young Applebaum. As am I."

The old man's chair rotated back toward the center of the arena, his amplified voice once again addressing the crowd. But the message had been delivered.

Billy nodded slightly, more to himself than anyone else. "Challenge accepted."

Back in their maintenance bay, Billy hunched over a workbench littered with scorched circuit boards and twisted metal components. The damage to The Reckoner was substantial—far worse than they'd initially assessed during the heat of battle.

"Power coupling's completely fried," he muttered, tossing the blackened component aside. "And the main hydraulic system took more strain than it was designed for."

Cristen sorted through a pile of salvaged parts they'd collected before the tournament. "We can rebuild the coupling, but we'll need to reinforce it. That last attack burned through almost everything."

"I knew Zoltar would recognize the power signature," Juno said, stepping out from the shadows. He'd changed back into more comfortable clothes, though he still looked uncomfortable among so much technology. "The Golden Node's energy pattern is distinctive."

Billy wiped grease from his hands. "He practically admitted he has my father."

"And now he knows you know," Relson added, returning from his reconnaissance around the arena perimeter. "Security's doubled since our match. They're watching us."

Zippy chirped anxiously from its perch on a nearby shelf, its sensors constantly scanning for surveillance devices.

"We've got eighteen hours before the semifinals," Billy said, pulling his father's goggles down over his eyes as he examined The Reckoner's damaged core. "Enough time to make repairs, but not enough to completely overhaul the systems."

Juno paced nervously. "You should withdraw. Zoltar's playing with you—he wants to see what the Node can do under pressure."

"That's exactly why we can't quit," Billy replied without looking up. "Dad's been his prisoner for years. This is our only chance."

Cristen placed a hand on Billy's shoulder. "We're with you, but Juno's right about one thing—Zoltar's expecting us now. We need a new strategy."

Billy finally straightened, a determined gleam in his eyes. "Then let's give him one. Relson, remember that old shield modulator you salvaged last month?"

Relson grinned. "The one you said was too unstable to use?"

"Exactly." Billy's fingers sketched a quick diagram on a nearby tablet. "What if instability is exactly what we need?"

Cristen leaned closer, studying Billy's diagram. "You want to overload the shield modulator? That's—"

"Crazy, I know." Billy's fingers traced the new configuration. "But if we route the Golden Node's energy through it in pulses rather than a continuous flow, we can create a feedback loop that looks like system instability to outside scanners."

Relson whistled. "A decoy. Make Zoltar think we're having power regulation issues."

"Exactly." Billy pointed to another section of the schematic. "Meanwhile, we'll be storing excess energy here, here, and here—distributed through backup capacitors instead of the main power core."

Juno shook his head, but there was grudging admiration in his eyes. "Hidden reserves. Your father used a similar trick in his third tournament."

"I saw it in his blueprints." Billy's expression softened briefly. "But I've modified it. Dad's version was defensive. Mine is..."

"A trap," Cristen finished, understanding dawning on her face.

Billy nodded. "Zoltar will be monitoring our power signatures. When he sees the fluctuations, he'll think we're vulnerable—maybe even expect us to break down mid-match."

"But really, you'll be charging up for something bigger." Relson grinned. "I like it."

Zippy chirped excitedly, swooping down to project additional schematics onto the workbench. The little drone had been analyzing The Reckoner's battle data, identifying weak points and suggesting reinforcements.

"We'll need to work through the night," Billy said, already sorting through components. "Relson, start on the shield modifications. Cristen, recalibrate the Node's interface to accept the pulse pattern. I'll rebuild the hydraulics with the distributed power system."

Juno watched them with a mixture of concern and pride. "And what about Zoltar's surveillance?"

Billy glanced at Zippy, who emitted a series of confident beeps. "Already handled. Zippy's broadcasting a loop of us making standard repairs—nothing suspicious."

As they dispersed to their tasks, Billy paused, looking up at The Reckoner's battle-scarred frame. In the dim light of the maintenance bay, the massive machine seemed to be watching over them—a silent guardian holding the key to his father's freedom.

"We're coming, Dad," he whispered. "Just hold on a little longer."

CHAPTER 15: FRACTURED TRIUMPH

Dawn filtered through the maintenance bay's high windows, casting long shadows across The Reckoner's gleaming frame. The night's frantic work had transformed the battle-worn machine into something new—something unpredictable.

"Power distribution systems online," Cristen announced, closing an access panel on the robot's left leg. Dark circles rimmed her eyes, but her movements remained precise. "Node interface is accepting the pulse pattern. We're getting ninety-two percent efficiency."

Billy nodded, tightening the last bolt on the modified hydraulic system. "Better than I expected. How's the shield coming, Relson?"

Relson emerged from behind The Reckoner's massive torso, his face streaked with grease. "Modulator's installed. It'll look like we're having intermittent failures, but the actual shield integrity will hold steady at seventy percent—just enough to take a beating without looking suspicious."

"And the capacitors?" Billy asked, climbing down from his perch.

"All six distributed power banks are charged and ready," Juno confirmed, checking readings on a diagnostic tablet. "Hidden exactly where no one would think to look."

He gestured to compartments built into The Reckoner's joints and back plating—places that would typically house only structural supports.

Zippy flew circles around the robot's head, scanning for any overlooked weaknesses. The little drone chirped in satisfaction before projecting the semifinal bracket onto the wall.

"Two hours until we face The Demolisher," Billy said, studying their opponent's specs. "Triple-reinforced armor plating, hydraulic crusher arms, and a reputation for disabling opponents in the first sixty seconds."

Cristen handed him a bottle of water. "Perfect for our strategy. The more aggressive they are, the faster they'll fall for our trap."

"Assuming Zoltar doesn't see through it," Juno cautioned. Billy took a long drink, then wiped his mouth with the back of his hand. "That's why we need one more modification." He pulled a small device from his pocket —a compact transmitter with his father's insignia etched into its casing. "This will broadcast a message directly to the arena's main systems when activated."

"What kind of message?" Relson asked.

Billy's expression hardened. "The truth. Dad's last recording, plus everything we've discovered about Zoltar. If we can't beat him in the ring, we'll beat him in public."

The arena's warning klaxon blared three times. Steel barriers rose from the floor, transforming the once-open battlefield into a labyrinth of obstacles. Concrete pillars, metal barricades, and half-demolished structures created a treacherous urban wasteland.

"Ladies and gentlemen," the announcer's voice boomed through the stadium, "welcome to the semifinal round! Introducing our first competitor—weighing in at eighteen tons of pure destruction, the undefeated champion of the Eastern Sector... The Demolisher!"

The crowd erupted as the squat, heavily-armored machine walked into the arena, its massive spiked fists rotating menacingly. Its demolition ball tail swung in wide arcs, smashing through a concrete barrier as if it were made of sand.

"And challenging today, the mysterious newcomer that's taken this tournament by storm—The Reckoner!"

Billy guided their towering creation through the entrance tunnel, feeling the vibration of thousands of spectators stamping their feet. The Reckoner's mismatched exterior gleamed under the arena lights, steam venting dramatically from its shoulder ports.

"Remember the plan," Cristen's voice came through his headset. "Let The Demolisher chase us through the obstacles. Wear him down."

"I know," Billy replied, maneuvering The Reckoner into position. His eyes flicked to the VIP observation lounge where Zoltar sat watching, surrounded by his entourage.

The countdown began.

"Three... two... one... FIGHT!"

The Demolisher charged forward with surprising speed, its tail whipping toward The Reckoner's legs. Billy sidestepped the attack, deliberately making the movement look clumsy and last-second.

"That's it," Juno coached through the comm. "Make him think you're struggling with the terrain."

The Demolisher pursued relentlessly, smashing through barriers to create a direct path. Its right fist slammed into The Reckoner's shoulder, sending their robot staggering backward into a pillar.

"Shields holding at sixty-eight percent," Relson reported.

"Perfect."

Billy guided The Reckoner in a strategic retreat, leading The Demolisher deeper into the maze of obstacles. With each exchange, he allowed their opponent to land glancing blows while The Reckoner appeared to weaken.

"He's falling for it," Cristen whispered. "Look at his power output—he's draining energy twice as fast as he should."

The Demolisher's tail swung again, this time connecting solidly with The Reckoner's midsection. The impact sent their machine crashing through a metal barricade.

Billy grimaced, feigning distress for the cameras while activating the hidden power capacitors in sequence.

"Now," he muttered. "Time to show them what real power looks like."

The Reckoner's systems hummed as the Golden Node's energy surged through its circuits. Billy's fingers danced across the controls, executing the maneuver they'd practiced countless times. The Reckoner dropped into a crouch, appearing to falter, drawing The Demolisher into overcommitting to its next attack.

"He's coming in hot," Relson warned. "Tail strike incoming at three o'clock."

The demolition ball whistled through the air. At the last possible moment, Billy activated the hydraulic boost. The Reckoner shot upward, clearing the attack by inches. The crowd gasped as the massive machine seemed to defy gravity.

"Now!" Billy shouted.

The Reckoner's enormous fist plunged downward, catching The Demolisher's tail mid-swing. With a violent twist, it wrenched the appendage from its housing. Sparks erupted as hydraulic fluid sprayed across the arena floor.

The Demolisher spun to face its attacker, but The Reckoner was already moving. It charged forward, pistons firing at maximum capacity, and delivered a thunderous uppercut that lifted The Demolisher's front end off the ground.

"Finish it!" Cristen urged.

Billy nodded, activating the final sequence. The Reckoner grabbed The Demolisher by both arms and, with a mechanical roar that shook the arena, ripped them clean off. The crippled machine teetered, then collapsed in a heap of twisted metal.

The crowd exploded in cheers as the buzzer sounded.

"Unbelievable!" the announcer screamed. "The Reckoner advances to the finals!"

But inside the control room, alarms blared. Red lights flashed across the diagnostic panels.

"Something's wrong," Juno said, his voice tight. "Power fluctuations throughout the system."

Cristen's fingers flew across the keyboard. "The main power regulator is failing—Node energy is backflowing into the primary circuits!"

The Reckoner shuddered in the middle of the arena, steam erupting from every joint. Inside the cockpit, displays flickered and died as circuit breakers popped in rapid succession.

"Shut it down!" Relson shouted. "Before we lose everything!"

Billy frantically initiated the emergency protocols, but it was too late. The main power regulator exploded in a shower of blue sparks, leaving The Reckoner frozen in victory pose as its systems went dark.

"We're dead in the water," Billy whispered, staring at the blank screens. "The finals are in twelve hours, and our regulator is fried."

The maintenance bay doors hissed open. Billy turned to see Zoltar himself entering, flanked by two security drones. The tournament organizer moved with a stiff, mechanical gait—his exoskeletal support system whirring softly with each step.

"Quite the predicament you find yourself in, young Applebaum," Zoltar said, his voice surprisingly gentle. "A spectacular victory followed by catastrophic failure."

Billy stepped protectively in front of his friends. "What do you want?"

"To offer a solution." Zoltar gestured, and one of his drones projected a hologram—schematics for an advanced power regulator, far more sophisticated than anything Billy had ever seen. "I have the only replacement capable of handling your... unique power source."

"And the catch?' Cristen asked, eyes narrowed.

Zoltar smiled thinly. "No catch. Simply an exchange of talent." He turned to Billy. "Join my engineering division. Tonight. Work alongside minds as brilliant as your own— as brilliant as your father's."

Billy's heart skipped. "My father?"

"Melvin is alive, of course. One of my most valued engineers." Zoltar's eyes gleamed. "Join me, and I'll take you to him immediately after the tournament concludes."

"And if I refuse?"

"Then you forfeit the finals. Such a shame after coming so far." Zoltar tapped his cane against The Reckoner's immobile leg. "I'm offering you everything you've been searching for—answers, reunion, and a future worthy of your talents."

Billy studied Zoltar's face, searching for deception. The

man's offer seemed too convenient, too perfectly timed. If Zoltar knew about the Golden Node, why not simply take it? Why negotiate?

A realization flickered through Billy's mind: Zoltar needed him for something. Something only Billy understood about the Node's integration with The Reckoner.

"I need time to think," Billy said carefully.

"Of course." Zoltar placed a small communication device on the workbench. "When you're ready to accept my generous offer, simply activate this. You have four hours before I require an answer." He turned to leave, then paused. "Oh, and Billy? Your father asked about you. Often. In the beginning."

The doors closed behind Zoltar, leaving Billy staring at the communicator, mind racing through possibilities. Not a rejection, not an acceptance—but perhaps an opportunity.

"We're not taking his deal," Billy said, snatching up the communicator and examining it. "This is a trap."

Cristen leaned against the workbench, arms crossed. "Obviously. But without a regulator, The Reckoner is just an oversized paperweight."

"What if we don't need it fully operational?" Relson suggested, pacing the length of the maintenance bay. "We just need Zoltar to think it is."

Billy's eyes lit up. "A shell game." He turned to Juno. "We could bypass the main regulator entirely and run minimal systems through the auxiliary power circuits."

"Enough to make it walk and look functional," Juno nodded, stroking his beard. "The diagnostics would show active systems, but we'd have no offensive capabilities."

"We don't need offensive capabilities," Billy said, climbing onto The Reckoner's leg to access a side panel. "We just need to get into the arena for the finals."

Zippy chirped excitedly, projecting schematics of The Reckoner's power distribution network onto the wall.

"If we reroute power from the secondary hydraulic systems," Billy continued, "we can maintain basic mobility and external lights. The steam vents can run on residual pressure."

Cristen caught on immediately. "A puppet show. Make it look alive enough to fool the entry scanners."

"And Zoltar's watching eyes," Relson added. "His security drones will be monitoring our every move."

Billy dropped down from his perch and grabbed his toolkit. "We've got four hours to make a dead robot look alive. Relson, start pulling the backup servos from storage. Cristen, we need to reprogram the diagnostic feedback to show false positives. Juno—"

"I'll work on a bypass circuit for the Golden Node," Juno finished, already pulling components from a nearby shelf. "We'll need to dampen its signature or Zoltar's sensors will detect the power inconsistency."

Zippy beeped a warning, displaying security camera footage of Zoltar's drones patrolling the corridor outside.

"They're watching," Billy muttered. "Good. Let them see us working desperately to fix The Reckoner. The more convinced they are that we're struggling, the less they'll suspect what we're really planning."

Billy stared at Zoltar's communication device, turning it over in his hands. The sleek black rectangle felt cold, almost predatory. He glanced at his friends, each working frantically on different parts of The Reckoner's systems.

"Time to decline his generous offer," Billy said, pressing the activation button.

The device hummed to life, projecting a small hologram

of Zoltar's face. The tournament organizer's thin smile appeared almost immediately.

"That was quick, young Applebaum. I take it you've made the wise choice?"

Billy squared his shoulders. "Actually, I'm declining. We've assessed the damage, and it's not as catastrophic as it first appeared. My team is already implementing repairs."

Zoltar's smile faltered slightly. "Are you certain? My engineers report your main power regulator was completely destroyed. Without it—"

"Without it, we'll have to get creative," Billy interrupted. "That's what engineers do, isn't it? Solve problems with the resources available."

"And your father? You're turning down the chance to see him after all these years?"

Billy's jaw tightened. "If I win this tournament fairly, I'll find him myself. If you have him, he'll still be there after I beat your champion tomorrow."

Zoltar's holographic eyes narrowed. "Bold words from a boy with a broken machine. Very well. I look forward to seeing these... creative repairs... in action." The hologram flickered out.

Billy immediately crushed the device under his boot. "He's definitely going to have this place under surveillance now."

"Already on it," Relson said, scanning for bugs with one of Zippy's peripheral devices. "Found three new ones in the last ten minutes."

Billy nodded, then looked up at The Reckoner's cockpit—currently open and exposed. "Cristen, we need to tint the cockpit glass. Maximum opacity."

"Won't that make it harder to see during the fight?" she

156

asked, already retrieving the necessary materials.

"That's the point. I don't want Zoltar's cameras seeing what we're doing inside once we're in the arena." Billy lowered his voice. "The less he knows about our actual control systems, the better our chances."

Juno understood immediately. "Smart. Make him think we're operating at full capacity when we're really running on fumes and tricks."

"Exactly," Billy said, helping Cristen apply the tinting film to the cockpit's transparent panels. "We need to control what Zoltar sees—and more importantly, what he doesn't see."

The maintenance bay transformed into a war room as midnight approached. Diagrams and hastily scribbled calculations covered every surface. Billy paced between workstations, his welding goggles pushed up on his forehead.

"So we get into the arena," Billy said, tracing their path on a projected map. "But how do we get from there to Zoltar's lab? The security will be tighter than ever."

Cristen tapped her bow against her palm. "We could create a distraction. Something big enough to draw attention away from the restricted areas."

"Like what?" Relson asked. "The Reckoner barely has enough juice to walk, let alone cause chaos."

Juno spread the arena schematics across the central table. "The problem isn't just getting to the lab—it's doing it while Zoltar is watching our every move. He'll know something's wrong the moment we deviate from the expected fight pattern."

"What if we don't deviate?" Billy suggested, eyes lighting up momentarily before dimming again. "No, that wouldn't work. We need to be in two places at once."

Zippy chirped excitedly, projecting a series of images showing the arena's underground maintenance tunnels.

"Service corridors," Cristen translated. "But they'll be guarded."

"And monitored," Juno added. "Zoltar's security system covers every inch of that facility."

Billy collapsed into a chair, rubbing his temples. "There has to be a way. The Reckoner can't actually fight tomorrow—we're basically sending a puppet into a chainsaw factory."

"What about the broadcast system?" Relson suggested. "Your dad's message—if we could hijack the arena screens —"

"We'd still need physical access to the main control hub," Billy countered. "Which puts us back at square one."

Zippy hovered near Billy's shoulder, beeping softly in what almost sounded like consolation.

"Maybe we're overthinking this," Cristen said. "What does Zoltar expect us to do?"

"Lose," Juno answered flatly. "Or take his deal."

"So we do neither," Billy muttered, staring at The Reckoner's immobile form. "But how?"

The room fell silent, each of them lost in thought, searching for the solution that remained frustratingly out of reach.

Billy confidently sits back in his chair and smiles mischievously. "I have an idea..."

CHAPTER 16: THE TROJAN GAMBIT

The arena pulsed with energy as the championship match approached. Spotlights swept across the massive circular battlefield, revealing scars from previous rounds —melted metal, oil stains, and deep gouges in the reinforced concrete floor.

The announcer's voice boomed through the stadium. "Ladies and gentlemen! The moment you've been waiting for! The championship battle for the Golden Circuit!"

On one side of the arena, Zoltar's champion—a sleek, obsidian machine called The Obliterator—entered with military precision. Its weapons systems hummed to life, pulse cannons extending from recessed compartments.

The crowd roared as the opposite gate creaked open. The Reckoner emerged, moving with surprising fluidity despite the extensive damage it had sustained in the previous round. Its mismatched metal frame caught the light in strange ways, rust and dents somehow making it look more formidable rather than weakened.

In the VIP box, Zoltar leaned forward, eyes narrowed. Something was different about The Reckoner's movements—more measured, more deliberate than before.

"Interesting," he murmured to his assistant. "Run a thermal scan on the cockpit."

"Sir, we can't. They've applied some kind of reflective coating to the glass. Our sensors can't penetrate it."

Zoltar's fingers tightened around his armrest. "Clever boy."

The Reckoner took its position, steam hissing from its vents as it settled into a combat stance. The cockpit remained completely opaque—a black mirror revealing nothing of what was happening inside. No silhouette of its pilot could be seen, no movement detected.

From the spectator stands, Cristen clutched her bow nervously. "Do you think it's working?"

Relson kept his eyes fixed on The Reckoner. "It better be. We've got one shot at this."

In the announcer's booth, the commentator was building anticipation. "The Reckoner has made a miraculous recovery after yesterday's devastating damage! But who's at the controls? Is young Billy Bolts still piloting after that crushing blow to their power systems? The cockpit's been completely blacked out—we can't see a thing!"

The countdown began. The crowd joined in.

"THREE!"

The Obliterator's weapons systems fully charged, glowing with deadly energy.

"TWO!"

The Reckoner shifted its weight, hydraulics whining.

"ONE!"

Both machines tensed, ready to launch forward.

"FIGHT!"

The Reckoner burst forward with unexpected speed, pistons firing in perfect sequence as it charged directly at The Obliterator. The crowd erupted, expecting a head-on collision between the titans.

The Obliterator's pilot took the bait. Serrated blades

extended from its arms, whirring to life as they swept horizontally across the arena floor—a deadly guillotine meant to slice through The Reckoner's head.

"He's going straight for the cockpit!" the announcer screamed.

At the last possible second, The Reckoner dropped into a slide, hydraulic joints compressing as it ducked beneath the lethal sweep of blades. Metal shrieked against metal as The Obliterator's weapons grazed The Reckoner's plating, sending sparks cascading across the arena floor.

The crowd gasped. This wasn't a normal combat maneuver.

The Reckoner skidded past its opponent, leaving The Obliterator slashing at empty air. But instead of turning to reengage, The Reckoner continued its momentum toward the far wall of the arena—directly at the maintenance access door used by repair crews between matches.

"What is this? The Reckoner's abandoning the fight! It's heading for the—"

The Reckoner's massive fist reared back, pistons extending to their maximum length. With a thunderous impact that shook the entire arena, it punched straight through the reinforced steel door, tearing a ragged hole approx 7 feet tall and 5 fit wide.

Concrete chunks and twisted metal scattered across the floor. Emergency alarms blared throughout the facility.

In the VIP box, Zoltar leapt to his feet. "Stop them! Lock down all maintenance corridors!"

A tremendous crash echoed through the arena as a massive metal plate tore free from The Reckoner's left leg, revealing the hollow interior. The panel hit the reinforced floor with a deafening clang that momentarily drowned out the blaring alarms.

"Go! Go! Go!" Billy shouted, emerging from the hidden compartment built into The Reckoner's leg. His welding goggles were pushed up on his forehead, eyes wide and alert as he scrambled toward the jagged hole in the maintenance door.

Cristen followed right behind him, her tech bow slung across her back. "So much for our stealth approach!"

"We never had stealth! We had distraction!" Relson tumbled out next, a backpack full of tools bouncing against his spine. "And it's working—look!"

The Obliterator had frozen in place, its pilot clearly confused by the unexpected turn of events. Security personnel were pouring into the arena from multiple entrances, but their attention was divided between the robots and the escaping teenagers.

Zippy zipped out last, chirping frantically as it darted in erratic patterns around the group, its yellow chassis flashing warning signals.

"I know, I know!" Billy replied to the drone's electronic chirps. "Thirty seconds until remote override fails!"

The four raced through the maintenance door, leaving The Reckoner standing motionless behind them. The robot had served its purpose—a Trojan horse that had gotten them inside the facility's restricted area.

"Remember the blueprints!" Cristen called out as they sprinted down a sterile white corridor. "First right, then second left!"

The hallway ahead was bathed in pulsing red emergency lights. Metallic shutters began descending from the ceiling—security protocols activating throughout the complex.

"Duck!" Relson shouted, sliding under the first

descending barrier just before it sealed the passage.

Billy and Cristen followed suit, rolling beneath the heavy metal door with inches to spare. Zippy barely squeezed through, one of its antennas getting clipped and bent backward.

Behind them, they heard the thunderous crash of The Reckoner finally collapsing, its remote control system failing as predicted. The sound of metal striking concrete reverberated through the walls, followed by the outraged roar of the crowd.

"My father's somewhere in this facility," Billy panted as they regrouped in the maintenance tunnel. "And we're going to find him."

Back in the arena, the supposedly disabled Reckoner suddenly twitched. Metal groaned as the massive machine's systems reactivated, hydraulics hissing as it pushed itself upright. The crowd's confused murmurs transformed into a deafening roar of disbelief.

"It's—it's getting up!" the announcer stammered, voice cracking with excitement. "The Reckoner is still operational!"

The Obliterator's pilot, convinced the match was already won, had turned his machine toward Zoltar's private box in a victory salute. The crowd's thunderous reaction was mistaken for adulation rather than warning.

Inside the VIP section, Zoltar gripped the railing, knuckles white. "What is happening? Who's controlling that machine?"

The Reckoner moved with purpose now, each step deliberate and heavy as it approached the oblivious Obliterator from behind. Steam vented from its joints, cooling systems working overtime as backup power cells surged electricity through its frame.

The arena screens displayed the Obliterator's pilot smiling confidently, waving to what he thought were adoring fans. His attention fixed on the crowd, completely unaware of the danger lurking behind him.

The Reckoner's massive fist retracted into its forearm, pistons locking into place. Titanium-alloy fingers clenched into a battering ram as it drew back for a devastating blow.

"LOOK OUT!" someone screamed from the stands, but the warning was lost in the cacophony.

With explosive force, The Reckoner drove its fist directly into the Obliterator's back, punching clean through layers of armor plating. The impact sent a shockwave across the arena floor, cracking concrete in a spiderweb pattern. Sparks erupted from the wound as The Reckoner's fist emerged from the front of the Obliterator's chassis, clutching critical components.

A catastrophic chain reaction followed—power cells rupturing, coolant lines severing, and control systems failing simultaneously. The Obliterator convulsed, electricity arcing across its frame before collapsing in a smoking heap of twisted metal.

Silence fell over the arena, broken only by the sizzle of melting circuitry and the heavy thud of the Obliterator's severed head hitting the ground. The Obliterator was thinly armored in the rear.

The Reckoner stood victorious over the smoking wreckage, steam billowing from its vents like a mechanical beast catching its breath. The crowd remained stunned, unsure whether to cheer for the unexpected victory or condemn the unorthodox tactics.

With a hydraulic hiss, the cockpit of The Reckoner began to open. Security forces rushed forward, weapons drawn, expecting to find Billy or one of his teenage accomplices. Instead, a familiar face emerged.

Juno Kett, The Caveman, rose from the pilot's chair, his clean-shaven face illuminated by the arena spotlights. He wore a proper jumpsuit now, not the ragged clothes of a man who'd lived in isolation for years. With surprising agility, he climbed onto The Reckoner's shoulder and raised both arms in triumph.

Recognition rippled through the crowd like a wave. First came gasps, then whispers, and finally a deafening roar that shook the very foundations of the arena.

"I DON'T BELIEVE IT!" The announcer's voice cracked with excitement. "LADIES AND GENTLEMEN, IT'S JUNO KETT! THE LEGENDARY CAVEMAN HAS RETURNED!"

The crowd's reaction intensified, years of speculation about his disappearance fueling their frenzy. Old fans who remembered his championship days were on their feet, pointing and shouting to younger spectators who had only heard the legends.

"THE FORMER CHAMPION HAS JUST DESTROYED THIS YEAR'S FAVORITE IN SPECTACULAR FASHION!" The announcer could barely contain himself. "BUT—BUT I'M BEING TOLD HE'S OFFICIALLY DISQUALIFIED! JUNO KETT IS NOT ON THE REGISTERED ENTRY LIST FOR THIS TOURNAMENT!"

Security forces hesitated, unsure how to approach the beloved figure as he basked in the adoration of the crowd. Even the booing at the disqualification announcement was half-hearted—the spectacle they'd witnessed overshadowed any technicalities.

Juno smiled broadly, soaking in the moment. His eyes swept across the arena to Zoltar's private box, where the tournament master stood rigid with fury.

"This is for you, Melvin," Juno said quietly, his words lost in the cacophony. "You've got an amazing son."

The quartet moved deeper into the facility's restricted section, navigating the labyrinth of sterile corridors. Emergency lights pulsed overhead, casting alternating shadows and crimson glows across their determined faces.

"Zippy, can you hack the security system?" Billy whispered, crouching at an intersection.

The small drone chirped affirmatively, extending a thin probe into a nearby access panel. Its eyes flickered rapidly as it processed data, then projected a holographic map onto the white wall.

"Perfect!" Billy traced a path with his finger. "Detention block is three levels down."

Relson peered around a corner, then quickly pulled back. "Guards. Two of them, armed with stun batons."

Cristen unsung her tech bow, fingers dancing across its interface. "I can create a distraction, but we'll need to move fast."

"Wait." Billy grabbed her arm. "No weapons unless absolutely necessary. Remember what my dad's message said—Zoltar doesn't just want robot engineers; he wants people who think like him."

Zippy chirped urgently, its antennae vibrating.

"Zippy's right," Billy translated. "There's another way." He pointed to a maintenance shaft barely visible behind a storage rack. "Service tunnel. It'll be tight, but we can make it."

Relson pulled the rack aside with surprising strength. "Ladies first."

Cristen rolled her eyes. "Such a gentleman." She slipped into the narrow passage, followed by Billy and Zippy.

Relson entered last, carefully pulling the rack back into position before squeezing through.

The shaft was claustrophobic—a metal tube barely three feet in diameter, filled with cables and pipes that hissed with steam. They crawled on hands and knees, guided by Zippy's soft blue glow.

"My father designed half these systems," Billy whispered, recognizing components. "See these coolant lines? That's his work—the efficiency pattern is unmistakable."

After several minutes of uncomfortable crawling, they reached a junction. Below them, through a ventilation grate, they could see a vast laboratory filled with partially assembled robots.

"Look." Cristen pointed to workers in identical jumpsuits, moving with mechanical precision between workstations. "Are those prisoners?"

Billy's breath caught. Each person wore a small device at the base of their skull—glowing with the same blue light as the facility's security systems.

"Neural inhibitors," he whispered, horror creeping into his voice. "They're being controlled."

Zippy suddenly emitted a series of urgent beeps, its body vibrating against Billy's side.

"What is it?" Relson asked.

Billy's eyes widened. "Zippy's picked up my father's biosignature. He's here! and he's close!"

The quartet navigated deeper through the network of maintenance tunnels, Zippy leading the way with occasional chirps and beeps that only Billy understood. The drone's antenna spun excitedly as it processed Melvin's biosignature.

"This way," Billy whispered, crawling faster. "He's on the next level down."

They reached an access panel that opened into a dimly lit corridor. The walls here were different—reinforced with a strange alloy that seemed to absorb sound. The floor beneath their feet hummed with barely perceptible vibrations.

"Secure laboratories," Cristen murmured, running her fingers along the wall. "High security."

Relson glanced nervously over his shoulder. "Too quiet. Where are the guards?"

"Maybe Juno's distraction is working better than we hoped," Billy replied, checking the schematic Zippy projected. "Dad should be in Lab 7, just around that corner."

As they approached the intersection, the overhead lights suddenly brightened to blinding intensity. A high-pitched whine filled the air as hidden speakers activated throughout the corridor.

"Welcome, Billy." Zoltar's voice boomed from every direction, smooth and cultured despite the undercurrent of menace. "I must commend you on your ingenuity. Truly impressive for one so young."

The group froze, backs pressed against the wall.

"You see, Billy—may I call you Billy?—I've been watching your progress with great interest. The modifications to The Reckoner were particularly inspired. Your father would be proud."

Billy's hands clenched into fists. "Where is he?" he says under his breath.

As if responding directly, Zoltar continued: "I understand your determination. The bond between father and son is powerful. But I fear you're setting yourself up for disappointment."

Zippy chirped anxiously, its sensors detecting movement

ahead.

"The man you seek is not the man you remember, Billy. Melvin has been in my employ for many years now. His mind has been... expanded. Enhanced. He's doing the work he was always meant to do."

Cristen grabbed Billy's arm as he started forward. "It's a trap," she hissed.

"Think carefully about your next move," Zoltar's voice softened to something almost paternal. "You've come so far, shown such promise. Why not join us? Your father's research awaits completion, and who better to assist him than his brilliant son?"

The speakers crackled with static before Zoltar's final warning: "Continue this foolish rescue attempt, and I promise you'll find only heartbreak at the end. Some things are better left undiscovered, Billy. Some truths are too painful to bear."

The corridor fell silent as Zoltar's voice faded, leaving only the low hum of machinery and the group's shallow breathing.

"He's lying," Billy whispered, his voice shaking with barely contained anger. "He has to be."

Relson peered around the corner, then quickly pulled back. "Two guards outside Lab 7. Armed with some kind of advanced stun rifles."

Cristen squeezed Billy's shoulder. "We need a plan. We can't just rush in."

Billy closed his eyes, forcing himself to think logically despite the emotions threatening to overwhelm him. His father was just beyond that door—so close after all these years. But Zoltar's words had planted a seed of doubt. What if his father had changed? What if he no longer wanted to be rescued?

"Zippy," Billy whispered. The drone hovered at eye level, its optical sensors fixed on Billy's face. "Run interference protocol."

The little drone chirped in acknowledgment, then zipped around the corner. Seconds later, they heard confused shouts from the guards, followed by the sound of equipment malfunctioning.

"Now!" Billy hissed.

They rounded the corner to find the guards frantically trying to reset their weapons as Zippy darted between them, emitting pulses that scrambled their electronics. Relson moved with surprising speed, tackling one guard while Cristen used her bow to trip the second.

Billy raced past the commotion, straight to the laboratory door. The security panel blinked red, denying access.

"Dad!" he shouted, pounding on the reinforced door. "Dad, it's me! It's Billy!"

The panel suddenly flickered, changing from red to green. The door slid open with a pneumatic hiss.

Billy stepped forward into the brightly lit laboratory, his heart hammering against his ribs. The room was filled with half-completed robotic components, holographic displays, and complex machinery that hummed with power.

And there, hunched over a workstation in the center of the room, was a man in a faded jumpsuit. He turned slowly, revealing a face older than Billy remembered, lined with years of captivity. But the eyes—those were the same eyes Billy saw every time he looked in a mirror.

"Dad?" Billy's voice cracked.

Melvin Applebaum stared at his son, recognition slowly dawning across his weathered features.

"Billy," he whispered. "You've grown so much."

CHAPTER 17: CHAINS OF THE MIND

Billy stepped forward, his legs suddenly unsteady beneath him. The moment he'd imagined countless times over the years was finally here, yet something felt wrong. His father's face showed recognition, but his eyes lacked the warmth Billy remembered.

"Dad... it's really you." Billy's voice trembled.

Melvin nodded mechanically. "You shouldn't have come here, son." His voice was flat, devoid of the passion that once animated his every word about robotics.

Billy glanced around the lab, taking in the advanced technology surrounding them. "We're here to rescue you. Mom's been waiting all these years."

"Rescue." Melvin repeated the word as if testing an unfamiliar concept. He turned back to his workstation without emotion. "That won't be necessary."

A chill ran down Billy's spine. This wasn't the reunion he'd pictured. Where was the bear hug? The tears? The excited questions about Billy's life?

"Dad, what did they do to you?" Billy approached cautiously, noticing the strange metallic implant at the base of his father's neck.

Melvin's hands continued working, assembling tiny components with inhuman precision. "Zoltar has shown me the true potential of human-machine integration. My work here is important."

Cristen and Relson entered the lab, securing the door behind them. They exchanged worried glances as they observed the strange interaction.

"That's not you talking," Billy insisted, fighting back tears. "The real Melvin Applebaum would never work for someone like Zoltar."

His father's movements paused for just a fraction of a second—so brief Billy almost missed it. A flicker of something crossed his face before the blank expression returned.

"The neural dampener requires recalibration," Melvin stated flatly, as if making a note to himself. "Emotional response detected."

Billy's mind raced. Neural dampener? The implant must be controlling his father somehow. The realization hit him like a physical blow—his father wasn't collaborating willingly. He was being manipulated, his emotions suppressed.

"Dad," Billy whispered, moving closer. "I'm going to get you out of here. Whatever they've done to you, we can fix it."

For an instant, Melvin's eyes cleared, a flash of the man Billy remembered breaking through. "Billy, you need to —" His words cut off abruptly as the implant at his neck pulsed with blue light. His expression went blank again, all trace of recognition vanishing.

Billy's hands clenched into fists, his knuckles white with tension. The enormity of what he faced crashed down on him all at once. This wasn't like fixing a broken droid or piecing together scrap parts. This was his father—transformed into something barely human by technology he couldn't begin to comprehend.

"I don't know what to do," Billy whispered, his voice cracking. The confidence that had carried him through the tournament evaporated. He wasn't the brilliant engineer who had built the Reckoner or the strategic pilot who had defeated combat robots twice his size. He was just a thirteen-year-old boy staring at the broken shell of his father.

His eyes burned with unshed tears. What had he been thinking? That he could waltz in here, find his dad, and they'd walk out together while Zoltar's minions just watched? The fantasy seemed childish now, embarrassingly naive.

"Billy?" Cristen moved closer, concern etched across her face.

"I can't do this." The words tumbled out before he could stop them. "I'm not... I'm not who everyone thinks I am. I'm just pretending." His shoulders slumped as he stared at the floor. "I'm not a hero. I'm not even a real engineer— I just copy what my dad did."

The weight of his inadequacy pressed down on him. All those nights spent studying his father's blueprints, all those hours in the combat arena—none of it had prepared him for this moment. The neural dampener on his father's neck might as well have been alien technology for all Billy understood about it.

"What if I make it worse?" His voice was barely audible now. "What if I try to remove that thing and it... it kills him?"

Billy looked at his hands—hands that could disassemble and reassemble complex machinery but now trembled with uncertainty. The gap between the boy he was and the hero he needed to be stretched impossibly wide.

A sharp sting jolted through Billy's arm. He whipped

around to find Cristen's fist still hovering in the air, her green eyes blazing with determination.

"Ow! What was that—"

"Snap out of it, Bolts." Her voice was steady, commanding. "This isn't the time for your pity party."

Billy rubbed his arm, indignation momentarily replacing his despair. "I'm not having a—"

"Yes, you are." Cristen stepped closer, lowering her voice. "Look, I get it. This is scary. But that man over there?" She nodded toward Melvin. "He needs the real Billy Applebaum right now. Not some whiny kid who gives up when things get hard."

Billy's mouth opened to protest, but Cristen pressed on.

"You need to find your inner calmness. Take a breath. Focus on the task at hand." Her expression softened slightly. "Ignore the noise, the pain, the self-doubt. All that garbage in your head telling you that you can't do this? It's lying."

Billy glanced back at his father, who continued working mechanically at his station, oblivious to their conversation.

"When you're tinkering with your bots, what do you do when you hit a problem you've never seen before?" Cristen asked.

"I... I slow down. Look at all the components. Find the pattern."

"Exactly." Cristen nodded. "So do that now. Focus, and the answers will reveal themselves."

Billy closed his eyes for a moment, forcing himself to take deep, measured breaths. The panic that had been building in his chest began to recede, replaced by a familiar clarity —the same feeling he got when facing a particularly challenging mechanical puzzle.

When he opened his eyes again, he studied the neural dampener with renewed purpose. The design, while advanced, followed logical engineering principles. There was a pattern there, waiting to be discovered.

"You're right," he said quietly. "Thanks for the reality check."

Cristen smiled. "That's what friends are for. Sometimes you need a punch in the arm to see clearly."

"You know," Cristen said, her voice softening as she watched Billy begin to analyze the neural dampener with renewed focus, "I've never been impressed by your robots."

Billy looked up, momentarily startled by her words.

"Wait, what? But you always said—"

"I mean, yes, they're incredible machines," she clarified, moving to stand beside him. "But that's not why I stuck around all these years."

Billy's hands paused over his father's implant. He turned to face her fully, confusion written across his features.

"Then why did you?"

Cristen smiled, a genuine warmth lighting her green eyes. "Because of who you are when things fall apart. When your inventions fail or blow up in your face—which happens a lot, by the way—you never quit. You get this look in your eyes, like the universe just handed you the most interesting puzzle ever created."

She gestured toward Melvin. "Your dad's situation isn't about having the right tools or knowing the perfect equation. It's about that stubborn, ridiculous heart of yours that refuses to accept defeat."

Billy swallowed hard, her words hitting something deep inside him.

"I believe in you, Billy Applebaum. Not because you

built a thirty-foot battle robot from scrap parts—though that was pretty cool—but because when that same robot crashed during our first test run, you picked yourself up and tried again."

She placed a hand on his shoulder. "That's who you are. Not just some genius kid who can build amazing things, but someone who faces impossible problems and doesn't back down."

Relson nodded from his position by the door. "She's right, man. I used to think you were just some weird tech nerd. But you're the real deal. You care about people, not just machines."

Billy felt something shift inside him—a quiet realization that perhaps his worth wasn't measured by his engineering skills alone. These people, his friends, saw something in him beyond his ability to build and fix things.

"Thanks," he whispered, the word inadequate for the emotion welling up in his chest.

Billy turned his attention back to the neural dampener attached to his father's neck. The device was smaller than his palm but clearly sophisticated—a marvel of miniaturized technology that made his own creations look primitive by comparison.

"Dad, I'm going to help you," he whispered, though Melvin gave no indication he heard. "Just hold on."

Billy leaned closer, careful not to touch the device yet. Its metallic surface had an iridescent quality, with microscopic patterns etched across the casing. Small blue lights pulsed rhythmically along its edge, matching what seemed to be his father's heartbeat.

"Zippy," Billy called softly. The small drone hovered forward from where it had been scanning the lab's perimeter. "I need you to analyze this neural dampener. Full spectrum scan, highest resolution."

Zippy chirped an affirmative and positioned itself carefully above Melvin's neck. A thin blue light emerged from the drone's underside, sweeping across the device in a precise grid pattern.

"Project the internal circuitry on that wall," Billy instructed, pointing to a blank section of the laboratory. "Magnify it so we can see everything."

Zippy processed for a moment, then projected a holographic display that filled the wall. The intricate circuitry of the neural dampener appeared in stunning detail—a complex maze of nanoscale components, power conduits, and what appeared to be biological interfaces.

Billy's eyes widened as he studied the projection. "This is incredible engineering," he muttered, tracing the paths with his finger in the air. "Look at how the neural inhibitors connect directly to the brain stem. It's not just controlling him—it's replacing parts of his autonomic nervous system."

The projection revealed something Billy hadn't expected: the dampener wasn't simply a control device. It was integrated with his father's nervous system so thoroughly that removing it incorrectly could cause catastrophic damage.

"It's like they've made his brain dependent on this thing," Billy said, his voice hushed with both awe and horror. "See these filaments? They're embedded in the neural tissue. Pull them out wrong, and..."

He didn't finish the sentence. He didn't need to.

Billy's mind raced as he studied the neural dampener's circuitry. The integration was sophisticated, but like all technology, it had to communicate with itself. Every system needed protocols, commands, handshakes...

"Wait a second," Billy murmured, leaning closer to the projection. "Look at this communication pathway. The dampener has to constantly verify its connection to maintain control."

His fingers traced the holographic circuit path. "It's sending a continuous authentication signal—like a heartbeat. The dampener is telling Dad's nervous system 'I'm still here, keep listening to me' over and over."

A plan began forming in Billy's mind, pieces clicking together like a complex machine assembly.

"Zippy," Billy called, excitement creeping into his voice. "Can you intercept and replicate the dampener's authentication signal?"

The drone chirped affirmatively, bobbing in the air.

"What are you thinking?" Cristen asked.

"We can't just remove the dampener—it's too integrated. But what if we trick it?" Billy's eyes lit up. "If Zippy can mimic the authentication signal and then gradually modify it to send a disconnect command..."

Billy turned to his drone. "Zippy, I need you to sync with the dampener's communication frequency. Once you've matched it perfectly, start inserting a modified authentication packet—one that includes a self-termination request."

Zippy hovered closer to Melvin's neck, extending a hair-thin antenna that positioned itself millimeters from the dampener. The drone emitted a series of soft, precise beeps as it worked to match the frequency.

"It's like speaking the dampener's language," Billy explained to Cristen and Relson. "We're going to make it think the disconnect order is coming from within its own system."

Zippy chirped excitedly, its display flashing green.

"Got it," Billy whispered. "Now, start sending the modified signal. Slowly—we can't trigger any security protocols."

The drone began its delicate work, infiltrating the dampener's communication system with surgical precision. On the wall projection, they could see the signal pattern shifting subtly as Zippy's counterfeit commands integrated with the authentic ones.

"It's working," Billy breathed, watching as the dampener's lights began to flicker in a new pattern. "The dampener thinks it's receiving a legitimate command to safely disconnect."

Melvin's body tensed suddenly, his back arching slightly as the neural dampener's lights flickered more rapidly. Billy froze, his heart hammering against his ribs.

"Is this supposed to happen?" Relson whispered, edging closer.

"I think so," Billy replied, though uncertainty crept into his voice. "The dampener is fighting back, trying to maintain control."

Zippy's antenna glowed brighter as it increased the signal strength, battling the dampener's resistance. The projection on the wall showed cascading changes through the neural pathways—like a dam beginning to crack under pressure.

"Dad," Billy whispered, "if you can hear me in there, fight it. Help us break through."

For several agonizing seconds, nothing happened. Then Melvin's fingers twitched. His shoulders shuddered. A small groan escaped his lips—the first genuine human sound Billy had heard from him.

"It's working!" Cristen exclaimed.

The dampener's lights suddenly flashed in an erratic

pattern, and Melvin's hand shot up to his neck. His eyes widened, clarity flooding back into them like a sunrise chasing away darkness.

"Billy?" His voice was hoarse, disbelieving. "Is that really you?"

"Dad!" Billy lunged forward, catching Melvin as he staggered. The neural dampener flickered once more before its lights went dark completely.

Melvin blinked rapidly, his eyes gradually focusing on his son's face. "You've grown so much," he whispered, raising a trembling hand to touch Billy's cheek. "Oh my God, you're my boy..."

"I'm here dad," Billy choked out, fighting back tears. "We've been looking for you."

Melvin's gaze darted around the laboratory, recognition and horror dawning on his face. "Zoltar... he's been using me. My designs. I couldn't stop myself." His voice cracked. "The things I've built for him..."

"It wasn't your fault," Billy insisted. "That neural dampener was controlling you."

Melvin touched the now-dormant device at his neck. "We need to remove it completely. The connection is temporarily severed, but it could reactivate."

"How do we do that safely?" Cristen asked.

"There's a medical bay two levels down," Melvin said, his engineer's mind already working through the problem. "It has the equipment we need."

Relson glanced nervously at the laboratory door. "We should move fast. Someone's bound to notice something's wrong."

As if on cue, an alarm began to wail throughout the facility. Red emergency lights bathed the laboratory in an ominous glow.

"Too late," Cristen muttered.

Melvin straightened, years of forced servitude giving way to determination. "Billy, listen carefully. Zoltar's planning something far worse than robot tournaments. He's building an army—combat droids designed for urban warfare."

"But why?" Billy asked.

"Power. Control." Melvin's face hardened. "He believes humanity needs to be governed by machines—his machines."

The laboratory door hissed, locks disengaging.

"We need to go,' Relson urged, backing away from the entrance.

Melvin grabbed Billy's arm. "Son, I'm so proud of what you've accomplished. The Reckoner—it's brilliant engineering."

Billy shook his head. "I just followed your blueprints."

"No," Melvin smiled, genuine pride in his eyes. "You improved them. Made them your own. You've become the engineer I always hoped you'd be."

The door began to slide open.

CHAPTER 18: ESCAPE FROM THE LABYRINTH

The laboratory door slid open with a hydraulic hiss. Six armed guards in black tactical gear stormed in, weapons raised and ready.

"Down! Everyone down now!" The lead guard shouted, his rifle trained on Melvin.

Billy ducked behind a heavy diagnostic console, pulling his father down with him. Cristen and Relson dove behind an adjacent workbench, narrowly avoiding the sweep of laser sights across the room.

"Find them!" The guard commander barked. "Zoltar wants the boy and his father alive. The others are expendable."

The guards spread out, methodically searching the lab. Heavy boots thudded against the floor as they moved between workstations. One guard approached their hiding spot, his shadow falling across the floor mere inches from Billy's foot.

Zippy hovered silently above a ceiling conduit, its optical sensors tracking the guards' movements. The little drone's processors calculated trajectories, power requirements, and probabilities in milliseconds.

Billy caught sight of Zippy and understood immediately. He grabbed his father's arm, squeezing it twice—their old signal for "be ready."

The guard's boots stopped directly in front of their hiding

place. "I think I found—"

Zippy dropped from the ceiling, its small frame suddenly expanding as panels opened along its sides. The drone emitted a high-pitched whine as it charged its emergency systems.

"Drone!" A guard shouted, swinging his weapon upward.

Too late. Zippy released a concentrated electromagnetic pulse that filled the room with blinding blue-white light. The guards' weapons sparked and went dead in their hands. Their tactical visors flickered and shut down, leaving them momentarily blind and disoriented.

"Now!" Billy shouted, grabbing his father's hand and bolting for the secondary exit.

Cristen and Relson followed close behind, weaving between the stumbling guards. One guard, recovering faster than the others, lunged for Cristen. She ducked under his grasp and Relson drove his shoulder into the man's midsection, sending him sprawling.

Zippy zipped past them, leading the way toward the exit, its small mechanical arms extended forward like a swimmer cutting through water.

"The pulse won't affect their comms for long," Melvin warned as they burst into the corridor. "We have minutes at most before reinforcements arrive."

Melvin stumbled, his legs still unsteady after years of confinement. Billy caught his father's arm, supporting him as they raced down the corridor.

"This way," Melvin gasped, pointing toward an unmarked section of wall. "There's a maintenance access point that leads to the service tunnels. They run beneath the entire compound."

Alarm klaxons began to wail throughout the facility. Red emergency lights pulsed along the ceiling, casting eerie shadows across their faces.

"How do you know about this?" Cristen asked, glancing nervously over her shoulder.

Melvin's face darkened. "Eight years in this hellhole. I memorized every inch I could access. Planned a hundred escapes in my head." He ran his fingers along a seemingly solid panel. "Never had the chance to try any of them until now."

His fingers found a slight depression in the wall. He pressed firmly, and a hidden panel slid back, revealing a narrow maintenance hatch.

"Zoltar keeps the main corridors heavily monitored, but these service tunnels are only checked during scheduled maintenance." Melvin crouched down, wincing as his stiff joints protested. "The security systems down there are minimal—designed to keep workers in line, not stop determined escapees."

Billy helped his father through the opening. The space beyond was tight—a cramped service corridor lit by dim emergency strips along the floor. Pipes and conduits ran along the ceiling, carrying power, data, and various utilities throughout Zoltar's compound.

"Zippy, take point," Billy whispered. The drone chirped softly and zipped ahead, its sensors scanning for threats.

Relson followed next, then Cristen. Billy came last, pulling the hatch closed behind them. It sealed with a soft click that sounded thunderous in the confined space.

"These tunnels were designed for maintenance drones," Melvin explained, his voice low. "Human technicians only use them when the automatics fail. We should be able to move through most of the compound undetected."

He paused, leaning against the wall to catch his breath. "But we need to hurry. Zoltar will figure out where we've gone soon enough."

A piercing alarm cut through the air, different from the general alert—higher-pitched, more urgent.

"That's the lockdown sequence," Melvin gasped, his face paling in the dim emergency lighting. "Zoltar's sealing the compound."

A thunderous mechanical groan reverberated through the service tunnel. Ahead, a massive blast door began descending from the ceiling, its reinforced metal edge slicing through the air with inexorable precision.

"Run!" Billy shouted, grabbing his father's arm and pulling him forward.

They sprinted toward the closing gap, boots pounding against the metal grating. The blast door continued its descent, the opening shrinking by the second.

Zippy shot ahead, easily clearing the narrowing space. Relson reached the door next, dropping into a baseball slide that carried him under the barrier with inches to spare.

"Cristen, go!" Billy pushed her forward as the gap narrowed to three feet.

She dove through the opening, rolling to her feet on the other side. The door continued its relentless descent.

"Dad, hurry!" Billy urged, practically dragging Melvin forward. The older man's face contorted with effort, his legs pumping as he pushed his body beyond its limits.

The gap shrank to two feet. Then eighteen inches.

Melvin reached the door first, dropping to his stomach and scrambling beneath the barrier. Billy followed immediately, flattening himself against the floor. The edge of the blast door scraped across his back, catching his tool belt for a heart-stopping moment before he wrenched himself free.

The door slammed shut with a final, definitive thud, sealing them off from their pursuers—but also from any easy retreat.

"That was too close," Relson panted, helping Billy to his feet.

Another alarm sounded, and ahead of them, a second blast door began to close.

"They're sealing all sections," Melvin warned. "Zoltar's trying to trap us between barriers."

They took off again, racing through the narrowing service tunnel. Ahead, blast doors were closing in sequence, each one triggered by the closure of the one before it.

"There!" Cristen pointed to a maintenance hatch in the ceiling just before the next closing door.

Zippy chirped frantically, hovering by the hatch. Its small mechanical arms worked the manual release as the group approached.

The hatch swung open just as they reached it. Relson laced his fingers together, creating a foothold for Cristen. She stepped into his hands and he boosted her up through the opening.

"Next section's almost sealed!" Billy warned, glancing back at the approaching blast door.

Cristen pulled herself through the hatch and scanned the dimly lit maintenance corridor. Her eyes narrowed as she spotted a security camera mounted in the corner, its red indicator light blinking steadily as it swept the area.

"Camera," she whispered down to the others. "Hold position."

She unfolded her tech bow with a fluid motion, the carbon-fiber limbs extending with a soft click. The weapon had been her constant companion since she'd modified it from salvaged parts three years ago. Unlike traditional bows, this one fired programmable micro-darts loaded with customizable payloads.

Cristen reached into the small pouch at her hip and extracted a specialized dart—matte black with a pulsing blue core. She nocked it against the bowstring, her fingers finding their familiar position.

The camera pivoted toward the hatch. In seconds, it would capture their escape route.

She drew back the string in one smooth motion, her breathing slowing as she tracked the camera's movement pattern. The bow's integrated targeting system projected a faint holographic trajectory line visible only to her.

"Ten seconds until the next blast door," Melvin warned from below.

Cristen didn't respond. Her focus narrowed to the camera and its predictable sweep. The targeting reticle in her vision flashed green as the perfect firing solution locked in.

She released the string.

The dart shot forward in absolute silence, crossing the distance in a heartbeat. It struck the camera's housing with pinpoint accuracy, magnetic clamps engaging instantly. The blue core pulsed once, twice—then released a localized EMP burst directly into the camera's circuitry.

The camera's indicator light flickered, then died. Its motorized mount froze mid-sweep.

"Clear," Cristen called down. "But we need to move fast. The system will flag the dead camera."

She reached down through the hatch, offering her hand to Billy's father. "The security grid will register this as a malfunction first, but they'll figure it out soon enough."

Relson crouched by the floor grate, examining the rusted

bolts that held it in place. The maintenance tunnel had narrowed, forcing them to move in single file through the cramped space. Overhead, pipes hissed with pressurized steam, casting the corridor in a warm, humid fog.

"According to the schematics I memorized, this vent should lead directly to the sub-level beneath the medical wing," Melvin whispered, his finger tracing an invisible path in the air. "If we can get there, we might find medical supplies and a less guarded exit route."

Relson pulled a multi-tool from his pocket, flipping open a pry bar attachment. "Stand back," he warned, wedging the tool into the seam around the grate. The metal groaned in protest as he applied pressure.

"This thing's completely seized up," Relson grunted, muscles straining. Sweat beaded on his forehead as he repositioned for better leverage. "Probably hasn't been opened in years."

Billy knelt beside him, examining the corroded edges. "The humidity in these tunnels has accelerated the oxidation process. The whole frame's fused."

Zippy hovered nearby, its sensors scanning the grate. The drone chirped a series of notes that only Billy understood. "Good idea," Billy nodded. He turned to Relson. "Zippy says we should try the corners first. The stress points will be weakest there."

Relson adjusted his approach, focusing on the upper left corner of the grate. He braced one foot against the wall and pulled with all his strength. The metal creaked, then gave way slightly.

"It's moving!" Cristen whispered excitedly.

Encouraged, Relson attacked the remaining corners in sequence, breaking the seal of corrosion at each point. With a final heave, the entire grate came free, revealing a dark vertical shaft below.

"Got it!" Relson grinned, his earlier fear replaced by determination. He set the grate aside and peered into the darkness. "Looks like about a fifteen-foot drop to the next level."

Zippy descended into the shaft, its built-in lights illuminating the way. The drone's sensors mapped the space, projecting a holographic display from its underbelly that showed the shaft's dimensions and the landing area below.

"Clear," Billy translated as Zippy returned. "The shaft opens into a storage room adjacent to the medical bay."

They descended the shaft one by one, using a series of maintenance rungs embedded in the wall. Zippy hovered nearby, casting just enough light to guide their way without attracting attention.

When they reached the bottom, they found themselves in a cramped storage room filled with decommissioned medical equipment. Dust-covered diagnostic machines and outdated surgical tools lined the walls, abandoned but not discarded.

"This way," Melvin whispered, leading them toward a service door at the far end of the room. "The medical wing should be through here, and beyond that, a maintenance corridor that leads to the exterior loading docks."

As they moved between the rows of equipment, Billy noticed his father's hands trembling. "Dad, are you okay? Do you need to rest?"

Melvin shook his head, his eyes darting nervously to the walls around them. "We can't stop. Not here." His voice dropped even lower. "Billy, there's something you need to know. Something I discovered during my captivity."

The group paused, huddling close in the dim light.

"Zoltar's been building an army," Melvin said, his face grim in Zippy's blue glow. "Not just combat robots for his tournaments—an actual mechanized army. Thousands of units, stored in a massive underground hangar beneath the arena."

Cristen's eyes widened. "An army? For what?"

"Global domination," Melvin replied. "The tournaments were never the end goal—they were a testing ground, a way to identify and capture the best engineers. We've been perfecting his war machines for him." He ran a shaking hand through his hair. "The final prototypes were completed six months ago. He's been mass-producing them ever since."

"How many?" Billy asked, his throat suddenly dry.

"Thousands. Maybe tens of thousands by now. Each one more advanced than anything the world's militaries possess." Melvin's voice cracked. "And I helped build them. My designs, my innovations—weaponized."

Relson swallowed hard. "So when we were fighting in the tournament..."

"You were unwittingly demonstrating combat techniques that his AI systems were studying and incorporating," Melvin finished. "Every match, every maneuver—it all fed into his learning algorithms."

"We need to warn people," Cristen whispered urgently.

Melvin nodded. "That's why escaping isn't enough. We need to find a way to disable that army before Zoltar activates it."

Zippy froze mid-air, its sensors suddenly alert. The drone emitted three short, staccato chirps—its warning signal.

Billy grabbed his father's arm, halting the group. "Patrol," he whispered, translating Zippy's alert. "Coming this way."

Zippy projected a small holographic map showing a squad of six guards moving through an adjacent corridor, their path converging with the group's position in less than thirty seconds.

"In here," Cristen hissed, spotting a narrow maintenance closet tucked between two massive diagnostic machines. She wrenched the door open, revealing a cramped space filled with cleaning supplies and spare parts.

They piled in, Melvin going first, followed by Relson and Cristen. Billy slipped in last, pulling Zippy with him and easing the door closed just as the distant sound of boots on metal flooring reached their ears.

The closet was suffocatingly small—barely four feet wide and six feet deep. Shelves lined with spare parts and maintenance tools pressed against their backs. A strong chemical smell permeated the air, a mixture of industrial cleaners and machine oil.

Relson's breathing quickened, his claustrophobia kicking in. Cristen placed a steadying hand on his arm, squeezing gently. He nodded gratefully, forcing himself to take slower, deeper breaths.

Billy held Zippy close to his chest, one hand covering the drone's optical sensors to prevent any telltale glow from escaping through the door's seams. The drone seemed to understand the need for absolute silence, its usual operational hum reduced to imperceptible levels.

The footsteps grew louder. Through the thin door, they could hear the patrol's communications.

"Section B-7 clear," a gruff voice reported. "Moving to medical storage."

"Copy that," came the reply over a comm unit. "Be thorough. Director Zoltar wants them found before they reach the outer perimeter."

The footsteps stopped directly outside their hiding place. A beam of light swept across the floor, visible through the gap beneath the door. The group held their breath, not daring to move a muscle.

"Check everything," the patrol leader ordered. "They could be anywhere."

Metal scraped against metal as the guards began searching the abandoned equipment. Something heavy crashed to the floor nearby, followed by a curse.

"Careful with that equipment," the leader snapped. "Some of it's still valuable."

The doorknob to their closet rattled. Billy felt his heart stop.

The doorknob turned slowly. Billy's fingers tightened around Zippy, his mind racing through escape scenarios —none of them promising.

A voice crackled over the patrol leader's comm unit. "All units, priority alert in Sector D. Possible intruder sighting. Converge immediately."

The doorknob stopped turning.

"Copy that," the patrol leader responded. "Squad Seven en route to Sector D."

The footsteps receded, fading down the corridor as the patrol rushed to respond to the false alarm. The group remained frozen for another full minute before Billy dared to crack the door open.

"Clear," he whispered, peering into the empty storage room.

They emerged from the closet, muscles stiff from the cramped quarters. Relson exhaled deeply, wiping sweat from his forehead.

"That was too close," Cristen murmured.

Melvin pointed toward a set of double doors at the far

end of the storage room. "The medical bay is through there. It should have emergency supplies and access to the maintenance corridor."

They crept across the room, careful to avoid disturbing the equipment. When they reached the doors, Billy pressed his palm against the access panel, hoping for a mechanical override.

Instead, a red light flashed, and a security prompt appeared on the small screen:

[SECURITY LOCKDOWN ACTIVE]

[AUTHORIZED PERSONNEL ONLY]

[BIOMETRIC VERIFICATION REQUIRED]

"It's electronically locked," Billy hissed, examining the security panel. "We need a staff member's credentials to get through."

Zippy hovered near the panel, scanning the interface. The drone chirped a complex sequence, its mechanical arms twitching with agitation.

"Zippy says it's a Class-4 security system," Billy translated. "Standard biometrics, but with additional lockdown protocols active. We can't spoof it with basic overrides."

Melvin knelt beside the door, examining the frame. "There's no mechanical bypass either. These medical bays are designed to be secure—to protect sensitive equipment and pharmaceuticals."

"Can we go around?" Relson asked, glancing back toward the storage room.

Cristen shook her head. "The schematics showed this as the only access point that isn't heavily monitored."

Billy's fingers drummed against his tool belt as he thought. "We need to hack it, but without triggering the security protocols."

He pulled a small device from his belt—a modified

diagnostic tool he'd built from salvaged parts. "This might work, but it's risky. If I get it wrong, we'll trigger every alarm in the facility."

CHAPTER 19: THE HEART OF THE MACHINE

Billy connected his diagnostic tool to the security panel, a mess of wires dangling between them. Zippy hovered nearby, its optical sensors fixed on the panel's inner workings.

"I need to trick the system into thinking we're authorized personnel," Billy muttered, fingers flying across the device's interface. "But these circuits are nothing like the ones I've worked with before."

Zippy chirped anxiously, its small mechanical arms extending toward the panel.

"What? No, that's too risky," Billy argued. "If we cross those connections—"

The drone beeped insistently, its body bobbing up and down for emphasis.

"Zippy's right," Melvin said, peering over Billy's shoulder. "The secondary verification protocol is separate from the main alarm system. If you isolate it first—"

"—then we can bypass the biometrics without triggering the facility-wide alert," Billy finished, eyes widening. "Zippy, you're a genius!"

The drone whirred happily, extending a thin probe from one of its arms.

"Hold the main circuit board steady," Billy instructed, carefully separating two bundles of wires. "I need to access the verification module without disturbing the alarm triggers."

Zippy's probe slipped into the narrow gap between components, its tip glowing faintly as it interfaced with the security system's core.

"Almost there," Billy whispered, sweat beading on his forehead as he rerouted power through his diagnostic tool. "Just need to—"

A harsh buzz emanated from the panel, followed by a flashing red light.

"No, no, no!" Billy hissed, frantically adjusting settings. "The security protocol is adapting!"

Zippy chirped in alarm, its probe flashing erratically as it fought against the system's countermeasures.

Distant alarms began to sound, growing steadily louder.

"They know we're here," Cristen warned, readying her tech bow.

"Billy, we need to move," Relson urged, glancing nervously toward the storage room entrance.

"Just... one... more..." Billy's fingers flew across his device, while Zippy's mechanical arms trembled with effort.

Suddenly, the panel emitted a soft chime. The red light switched to green, and the heavy doors slid open with a pneumatic hiss.

"Got it!" Billy exclaimed, disconnecting his tool as Zippy retracted its probe.

The alarms continued to blare, echoing through the facility's corridors.

"We bypassed the door security, but not the motion sensors inside," Billy explained, gathering his equipment. "They know someone's breached this section."

The group rushed into the medical bay, a sterile white room filled with advanced equipment. Holographic displays flickered to life as they entered, bathing everything in a soft blue glow. Melvin scanned the room, recognition flashing in his eyes.

"This is where they installed it," he whispered, touching the back of his neck where the neural dampener sat beneath his skin. "They kept me conscious during the procedure. Wanted me to understand exactly what they were doing to my mind."

Billy's face hardened. "We'll get it out, Dad."

Melvin nodded, then pointed to a series of cabinets along the far wall. "Cristen, Relson—we need surgical tools. Look for a laser scalpel and tissue regenerator in the drawers marked with red symbols."

Cristen moved immediately, pulling open drawers with practiced efficiency. "What else? I've watched a lot of surgeries on the Holovision. Lets do this."

"Neural interface scanner," Melvin replied, leaning against an examination table for support. "It's about the size of your palm, with three extending probes. Should be in a case with the Zoltar Industries logo."

Relson hesitated, eyeing the unfamiliar medical equipment with apprehension.

"You'll know it when you see it," Melvin assured him. "The scanner has a holographic display that maps neural pathways. We need it to locate the dampener's connection points before extraction."

Relson nodded and began searching through a tall storage unit. "This stuff looks expensive."

"And dangerous in the wrong hands," Melvin added. "Which is why Zoltar kept it all to himself."

Cristen held up a sleek metallic device. "Is this the laser scalpel?"

"Yes, perfect," Melvin confirmed. "Now find the tissue

regenerator—it looks similar but with a blue activation strip instead of red."

The alarms continued to blare throughout the facility. Zippy darted to the entrance, extending a small antenna to monitor approaching threats.

"Hurry," Billy urged, helping his father onto the examination table. "Zippy says we've got security converging on this level."

Relson pulled open a locked cabinet, revealing a black case emblazoned with the Zoltar Industries logo. "Found it!"

"Bring everything here," Melvin instructed, lying back on the table. "We don't have much time."

As Relson handed the neural scanner to Billy, a sharp crackle emanated from the medical bay's overhead speakers. The group froze, tools in hand, as Zoltar's unmistakable voice filled the room.

"How touching," Zoltar's voice oozed through the intercom, dripping with condescension. "The prodigal son returns to rescue daddy dearest."

Billy's grip tightened around the scanner, knuckles whitening. "He can see us."

"Indeed I can, young Applebaum. Did you really think I wouldn't have special surveillance in my medical facilities?" Zoltar chuckled, the sound distorted and hollow through the speakers. "I've been watching your little adventure with great amusement."

Melvin struggled to sit up on the examination table. "Don't listen to him, Billy."

"Oh, but he should," Zoltar continued. "You see, Billy, what you're attempting is quite impossible. Your father's neural dampener isn't just a simple device that can be removed like a splinter. It's integrated with his central nervous system—has been for years now."

Billy looked at his father, uncertainty flickering across his face.

"The neural pathways have been permanently altered," Zoltar explained, his voice almost sympathetic. "Even if you somehow managed to extract the physical component—which you won't—the damage is irreversible. His mind has been rewired, reconfigured to serve my purposes."

"You're lying," Billy spat, though his voice wavered.

"Am I? Ask him about the headaches. The blackouts. The moments when his thoughts simply... vanish. That's not the dampener, boy. That's what happens when you try to think against your programming."

Melvin's expression darkened. He avoided Billy's questioning gaze.

"Your father's brilliance serves me now," Zoltar continued. "It has for years. Whatever spark of rebellion brought him to record that message was merely a glitch —one I've since corrected. The man you're trying to save doesn't exist anymore."

Billy's hands trembled as he stared at the neural scanner's display. The complex web of connections between the dampener and his father's brain stem appeared impossibly intricate.

"Face reality, Billy," Zoltar's voice softened to a patronizing whisper. "You can't undo what's been done. The father you remember is gone."

"He's trying to get in your head," Billy said, fighting to steady his hands. "Just like he did with that thing in your neck."

Melvin reached up, gripping his son's wrist. "The scanner, Billy. Focus on the scanner."

Billy nodded, pushing aside Zoltar's taunts. He activated

the neural interface scanner, its three probes extending with a soft mechanical whir.

"Hold it about two centimeters above the base of my skull," Melvin instructed, turning to lie face-down on the examination table. "The dampener sits between the C1 and C2 vertebrae, anchored to the medulla oblongata."

Billy positioned the scanner as directed, watching as a three-dimensional holographic model materialized above the device. Neural pathways appeared as glowing blue filaments, while the dampener showed as an angry red mass embedded within them.

"What am I looking at, Dad?" Billy asked, adjusting the scanner to sharpen the image.

"The dampener has primary and secondary connection points," Melvin explained, his voice strained from the awkward position. "The primaries control motor function and speech—those are the thick red lines branching upward. The secondaries—those finer filaments spreading outward—suppress independent thought and memory retrieval."

Zippy hovered closer, beeping softly as it analyzed the holographic display.

"Zippy's right," Billy murmured. "These connection patterns look familiar. Like the circuit designs in your old blueprints, but... organic."

"Because they're based on my own neural architecture," Melvin confirmed. "Zoltar forced me to design it that way. The dampener adapts to the host's brain patterns, making it nearly impossible to remove without causing permanent damage."

Billy rotated the scanner slightly, revealing more of the complex web. "Nearly impossible isn't the same as impossible."

The hologram flickered as Billy adjusted the scanner's sensitivity. Suddenly, a new pattern emerged—a series of pulsing nodes along the dampener's perimeter.

"What are these?" Billy asked, indicating the nodes.

Melvin squinted at the display. "Control junctions. They regulate the dampener's intensity based on... based on..." He faltered, wincing as pain flashed across his face.

"Dad?"

"It's fighting me," Melvin gasped. "When I try to access certain memories, the dampener activates. But I can see the pattern now. Billy, if we can isolate those junction points in sequence, we might be able to deactivate it before removal."

Relson backed away from the door, his eyes darting frantically between the corridor outside and the medical equipment lining the walls.

"They're coming," he hissed, rushing to a tall diagnostic unit mounted on wheels. "We need to buy time!"

He threw his weight against the heavy machine, grunting with effort as it slowly slid across the polished floor. The unit's screen flickered and died as he wrenched it free from its power coupling.

"Help me with this!" Relson called to Cristen, who immediately abandoned her position by the surgical tools.

Together they shoved the massive unit against the door, its metal frame scraping loudly against the floor. The sound of approaching footsteps grew louder —disciplined, rhythmic boots striking the corridor in unison.

"Not enough," Relson muttered, scanning the room. His eyes locked on a reinforced cabinet filled with medical supplies. "That one!"

He and Cristen wrestled the cabinet away from the wall, cables snapping as they dragged it across the room. With a final heave, they tipped it against the diagnostic unit, creating a makeshift barrier.

"Still not enough," Relson panted, sweat beading on his forehead. "They'll blast through this in seconds."

The footsteps halted just outside. Muffled voices exchanged commands.

Relson grabbed a surgical table, upending it with a crash of scattered instruments. He wedged it sideways into the growing barricade, metal legs scraping against the door frame.

"The oxygen tanks," Melvin called from the examination table, pointing to a rack of pressurized cylinders. "Careful —they're explosive under the right conditions."

Relson nodded grimly, dragging two of the heavy tanks to reinforce the lower portion of their barrier. He positioned them strategically, ensuring the valves faced away from the door.

"If they start cutting through," he explained to Cristen, "we can use these as a last resort."

A harsh electronic buzz sounded from the other side of the door—security override codes being entered.

"That won't hold them for long," Relson warned, stepping back to survey their hasty fortification. "Maybe a minute, two at most."

The door mechanism whirred and clicked as it attempted to slide open, straining against the weight of the barricade. Metal groaned under pressure.

"I'm ready," Melvin whispered, gripping the edges of the examination table. "The junction points need to be deactivated in sequence—lateral to medial, following the natural neural pathway."

Billy positioned the laser scalpel above the first junction point, its tip glowing faintly red. Zippy hovered nearby, projecting the holographic scan directly above Melvin's exposed neck.

"Start with the outermost connection," Melvin instructed, his voice steady despite the pounding at the door. "A two-second pulse, no more."

Billy's hand trembled slightly. "If I miss—"

"You won't," Melvin assured him. "Your hands are steadier than mine ever were."

Taking a deep breath, Billy activated the scalpel. A thin beam of concentrated light pierced the skin at the base of Melvin's skull, targeting the first junction point with surgical precision. Melvin tensed but remained still.

"First junction deactivated," Billy announced as the holographic display showed the connection point fading from red to blue. "Moving to the second."

The barricade at the door shuddered as something heavy slammed against it from the other side. Metal screeched against metal.

Billy repositioned the scalpel, targeting the second junction point. Another pulse, another connection severed. The hologram updated in real-time, showing the dampener's grip loosening.

"Third junction," Billy murmured, shifting the scalpel slightly.

As the beam touched the third connection point, Melvin's body suddenly went rigid. His back arched violently, limbs thrashing against the examination table.

"Dad!" Billy cried, yanking the scalpel away.

Melvin's eyes rolled back, his jaw clenched in a silent scream. His entire body convulsed, muscles spasming uncontrollably.

"What's happening?" Cristen rushed to help hold Melvin down, her face pale with shock.

"The dampener—it's fighting back!" Billy's voice cracked with panic as he struggled to stabilize his father. "It's triggering some kind of defense mechanism!"

Melvin's convulsions intensified. A thin trickle of blood seeped from his nose, bright red against his ashen skin.

"We have to stop!" Cristen pleaded, struggling to keep Melvin's thrashing arms from injuring himself.

"If we stop now, we might not get another chance," Billy argued, though horror filled his eyes as his father's body bucked violently beneath his restraining hands.

Zippy darted frantically around them, its sensors blinking rapidly as it analyzed Melvin's deteriorating vital signs. The drone emitted a series of urgent, high-pitched beeps.

"His neural patterns are destabilizing," Billy translated, his voice hollow with fear. "The dampener is overwhelming his central nervous system."

Melvin's convulsions suddenly ceased. His body went limp, eyes fluttering open as clarity returned to his gaze. The holographic display above his neck pulsed once, twice—then the angry red mass representing the dampener flickered and dimmed to a dull amber.

"Billy," Melvin gasped, his voice stronger than it had been since their reunion. "It's... receding."

Billy stared at the display in disbelief. "The neural pathways are... regenerating? How—"

"The Golden Node," Melvin whispered, slowly pushing himself upright. "Its energy signature must have interfered with the dampener's control matrix. Your power source saved me."

Billy helped his father sit up, supporting his shoulders as

Melvin swung his legs over the edge of the examination table. Blood still trickled from his nose, but his eyes were clear—sharper and more focused than before.

"Dad, are you really—"

"It's me, son," Melvin said, his voice breaking. "For the first time in years, it's really me."

Billy's face crumpled, years of longing and grief surging to the surface. Melvin pulled him into a fierce embrace, his arms trembling not from weakness but from the overwhelming emotion of holding his son again.

"You never gave up," Melvin whispered, tears streaming down his weathered face. "All these years. You never stopped looking."

Billy clutched his father tightly, burying his face against Melvin's shoulder. "I had to find you. I had to know."

"You did more than find me," Melvin choked out. "You saved me. You brought me back."

The barrier at the door groaned as security forces redoubled their efforts to break through. Metal twisted and buckled under the assault.

"We need to move," Relson urged, his eyes fixed on the weakening barricade.

A deafening explosion rocked the corridor outside, the concussive force shaking the entire medical bay. Dust and debris rained from the ceiling as the lights flickered. The barricade held, but barely—now protecting them from whatever chaos had erupted in the hallway.

"What was that?" Cristen gasped, steadying herself against a cabinet.

Melvin pulled back from the embrace, keeping one arm firmly around Billy's shoulders as he wiped tears from his eyes.

"That," he said with a ghost of a smile, "might be our way

out."

CHAPTER 20: THE ARMY AWAKENS

"Emergency exit," Melvin pointed to a narrow doorway half-hidden behind a supply cabinet. "Every medical facility has one—building code."

Relson shoved the cabinet aside, revealing a reinforced door with a simple mechanical release lever. No electronics, no security protocols.

"Old school," Relson grinned, pulling the lever down with a satisfying clunk. The door swung open to reveal a dimly lit maintenance passage.

"Freight access,' Melvin explained as they filed through. "Connects to the service elevator shaft."

Another explosion rocked the facility, closer this time. The lights in the passage flickered and died, plunging them into darkness before emergency strips along the floor activated, casting an eerie red glow.

"Zippy, scan ahead," Billy instructed.

The little drone zipped forward, its sensors sweeping the passage before returning with a series of confident beeps.

"Clear for now," Billy translated. "Elevator shaft is thirty meters ahead."

They moved quickly through the narrow corridor, Melvin leaning on Billy's shoulder. Though the neural dampener's control had been broken, years of inactivity had left Melvin's muscles weak.

"I can hear it," Cristen whispered as they approached the end of the passage. "Below us."

They all paused, listening. A deep mechanical hum vibrated through the floor, punctuated by rhythmic clanking and the hiss of hydraulics.

"The army," Melvin confirmed grimly. "Zoltar's been mass-producing combat droids. Hundreds of them."

The service elevator stood before them, its doors pried partially open from some previous malfunction. Through the gap, they could see the vast shaft descending into darkness.

"Down there?" Relson peered through the gap, his face illuminated by the red emergency lighting. "That's the hangar level?"

Melvin nodded. "Four levels down. That's where Zoltar keeps his war machines."

Billy examined the elevator's manual override. "The car is stuck two levels below us. We'll have to climb down the maintenance ladder to reach it."

"Then what?" Cristen asked.

"Then we ride it the rest of the way down," Melvin said, his voice hardening with resolve. "And we end this."

The mechanical symphony from below grew louder, more insistent. The floor beneath their feet vibrated with increasing intensity.

"They're powering up," Melvin warned. "We don't have much time."

Billy pried the elevator doors fully open, and they descended the maintenance ladder in silence, the only sound their breathing and the occasional creak of metal. When they reached the stalled elevator car, Relson forced the hatch open, and they dropped inside one by one.

"Manual override here," Melvin pointed to a panel beneath

the control board. Billy yanked it open and connected Zippy to the circuitry. The little drone's eyes flickered as it interfaced with the elevator's systems.

The car jerked to life, descending slowly toward the hangar level. The mechanical symphony grew louder, a cacophony of industrial sounds that vibrated through the walls.

"Ready yourselves," Melvin whispered as the elevator slowed. "What you're about to see—"

The doors slid open.

Billy stepped forward and froze. The vast underground hangar stretched before them, a cavernous space larger than the arena above. Row upon row of combat droids stood in perfect formation, motionless yet somehow alert. Their sleek, angular bodies gleamed under harsh industrial lighting, chrome and matte black surfaces reflecting the movement of automated assembly arms that continued to work on the outer ranks.

"My designs," Melvin breathed, his voice hollow with horror. "All my designs."

Each droid stood three times human height, bipedal but with multiple auxiliary limbs folded against their torsos. Their featureless heads housed sensor arrays more advanced than anything Billy had ever seen. Where The Reckoner had been built with scraps and passion, these machines were precision-engineered weapons of war.

"There must be hundreds," Cristen whispered.

"Five hundred and twelve," Melvin corrected, his engineer's eye automatically counting. "Plus the assembly line is still active."

Billy recognized elements from his father's blueprints in each machine, but twisted, weaponized beyond recognition. What had been created for protection and competition had been perverted into instruments of conquest.

"This is what he wanted me for," Melvin said, his voice breaking. "Why he kept me alive all these years. My mind, my designs..."

A rhythmic pulsing light swept across the ranks of droids, bathing them in crimson. Along the far wall, status indicators began switching from amber to green.

"They're initializing," Billy realized with growing dread.

"Citizens of our glorious nation!"

The booming voice echoed through the hangar as spotlights swiveled upward, illuminating a platform high above the assembly floor. Zoltar stood at its edge, arms spread wide in theatrical triumph. His white hair formed those distinctive three peaks, and his frail body was supported by an exoskeleton that gleamed with the same technological signature as the droids below.

"Behold the dawn of a new era!"

Six elite guards flanked him, their uniforms a stark contrast to the standard security forces—matte black armor with pulsing circuitry that matched the combat droids. Their faces were obscured behind polarized visors, but their posture conveyed absolute loyalty.

"For too long, our society has suffered under the illusion of freedom," Zoltar continued, his voice amplified throughout the chamber. "Chaos masquerading as choice. Disorder disguised as democracy."

The assembly line accelerated, robotic arms working at frenzied speed to complete the final units.

"Tonight, at precisely midnight, my peacekeeping force will deploy to every major city. By dawn, a new order will be established—my order, a globalist order."

Billy and his companions pressed back against the

elevator wall, momentarily forgotten in Zoltar's moment of triumph.

"Each droid is equipped with advanced tactical systems and non-lethal compliance measures. The transition will be swift and—for those who accept their place—painless."

Zoltar's gaze swept across the hangar floor, his eyes narrowing as they landed on the small group by the elevator.

"Ah, the Applebaums. Father and son, reunited at last." His thin lips stretched into a smile that never reached his eyes. "How touching that you've arrived to witness the culmination of Melvin's life's work."

One of the elite guards stepped forward, weapon raised.

"No," Zoltar held up a hand. "Let them watch. Let them understand the futility of resistance before the end."

The first row of combat droids activated fully, their sensor arrays glowing with cold blue light as they stepped forward in perfect unison.

"The deployment countdown has begun," Zoltar announced. "In thirty minutes, my army marches forth to restore order to a world drowning in its own freedom."

Melvin's eyes darted across the hangar, analyzing the layout with the precision of a seasoned engineer. His gaze locked onto a cylindrical structure at the center of the droid formation—a massive pillar surrounded by pulsing conduits that fed into each machine.

"The synchronization hub," he whispered, leaning close to Billy. "See that central node? It's coordinating the entire army through a quantum entanglement matrix."

Billy followed his father's gaze. The node glowed with an unearthly blue light, energy coursing through transparent tubes into each droid.

"One system controlling them all," Billy murmured. "Single point of failure."

"Thank goodness the good guys use decentralized tech." Billy utters softly.

Melvin nodded. "Zoltar always did prefer elegant solutions. Efficient, but vulnerable." He gripped Billy's shoulder. "You and Zippy can disable it. The access panel requires biometric authentication, but—"

"But Zippy can spoof the signal," Billy finished, already understanding.

"I'll create a distraction," Melvin said, straightening his posture despite his weakened state. "Draw Zoltar's attention. He's always had a flair for the dramatic—he won't be able to resist gloating over his former protégé."

"That's suicide," Cristen hissed.

"Not if we time it right," Melvin countered. "Relson, Cristen—when the alarm sounds, head for the eastern exit. There's an emergency vehicle bay."

Billy's heart hammered against his ribs. "Dad—"

"Trust me, son." Melvin's eyes shone with newfound clarity. "You built The Reckoner from scraps. This?" He gestured at the control node. "This is just another machine waiting to be taken apart."

Zippy chirped softly, hovering at Billy's shoulder.

"Follow the maintenance crawlway," Melvin pointed to a narrow service passage running along the wall. "It'll lead you behind the assembly line. You'll be in Zoltar's blind spot."

Billy swallowed hard, then nodded. "What's the shutdown sequence?"

"Overload the quantum buffer. The failsafes will trigger, but Zippy can bypass them." Melvin tapped the drone gently. "Just like we used to do with the old CompuCore systems, remember?"

Zippy beeped affirmatively.

"I'll see you on the other side," Melvin promised, his voice steady. Before Billy could respond, his father stepped out from their hiding place, arms raised.

"Zoltar!" Melvin called out, his voice echoing through the hangar. "Still hiding behind machines, I see!"

Cristen grabbed Relson's arm as they watched Melvin stride forward. "We need to buy Billy time."

Relson nodded, scanning the hangar. His eyes locked on a maintenance cart stacked with tools. "There. Equipment we can use."

They slipped along the wall, keeping to the shadows as Zoltar's attention fixed on Melvin. The guards' heads turned, tracking Melvin's bold approach, momentarily ignoring the other intruders.

"On three," Cristen whispered, unslinging her tech bow. "One... two..."

Relson darted toward the cart, snatched up a pneumatic wrench, and hurled it at the nearest security panel. The panel exploded in a shower of sparks, alarms blaring instantly.

"Intruders in Sector Seven!" a mechanized voice announced. "Security breach!"

Three guards broke formation, rushing toward them with weapons drawn. Cristen loosed an arrow—not at the guards, but at the overhead lighting array. The arrow detonated with a brilliant flash, plunging their section of the hangar into darkness.

"Can't hit what you can't see!" Relson taunted, grabbing more tools from the cart.

A guard lunged through the darkness, thermal visor glowing red. Relson ducked under his swing and jammed a screwdriver into the joint of the guard's armor. The man howled, his suit's systems shorting out.

Cristen rolled behind a storage container as energy bolts sizzled past her. She nocked another arrow, this one loaded with an EMP charge, and fired at the feet of the approaching guards. The pulse knocked out their suit systems, leaving them staggering in suddenly deadweight armor.

"The maintenance bay!" she called to Relson, pointing toward a side passage.

Relson grabbed a welding torch from the cart, ignited it, and swept it in a wide arc to keep the recovering guards at bay. "Go! I'll cover!"

More guards poured in from a side entrance. Cristen fired rapid shots, her arrows deploying smoke screens and sonic disruptors that threw the reinforcements into confusion.

Relson upended the heavy cart, sending tools skittering across the floor—creating a field of rolling hazards that sent two guards crashing down. He backed toward Cristen, wielding the torch like a sword.

"Not bad for a couple of kids," he grinned, dodging an energy bolt that scorched the wall behind him.

"Less talking, more running!" Cristen grabbed his collar, yanking him through the maintenance bay doors as she fired her last arrow at the control panel, jamming it shut behind them.

Billy crawled through the maintenance shaft, Zippy floating silently beside him. His heart pounded in his ears, drowning out the distant sounds of combat where his father, Cristen, and Relson fought to buy him time. The narrow passage opened onto a maintenance platform behind the central node—exactly where his father said it would be.

The quantum synchronization hub towered before him, a pillar of pulsing blue light and complex circuitry. Up close, it was massive—at least fifteen feet tall, with dozens of connection points feeding power and commands to Zoltar's army.

"Okay, Zippy," Billy whispered, hands trembling as he surveyed the access panel. "Just like Dad said."

Zippy chirped softly and extended a thin probe, interfacing with the biometric scanner. The panel flashed red, then green, sliding open to reveal a bewildering array of controls and circuit pathways.

Billy's confidence faltered. This wasn't some scrapped droid or salvaged tech he could tinker with in his workshop. This was cutting-edge military hardware, designed by geniuses with unlimited resources.

"What am I doing?" he murmured, hands hovering uncertainly over the controls. "I build toys from junk. This is..."

The enormity of what he faced crashed down on him. Five hundred war machines. A madman's vision of global domination. His father's freedom. His friends' lives. All hanging on his ability to disable technology he barely understood.

His fingers froze above the circuit board. What if he triggered a security protocol? What if the failsafes were beyond Zippy's capabilities? What if his tampering accelerated the deployment instead of stopping it?

Zippy nudged his hand, beeping questioningly.

"I can't," Billy whispered, a cold sweat breaking out across his forehead. "I'm just a kid playing with scraps. This is real. If I mess this up..."

The countdown timer on the hub's display continued its

relentless descent: 18:42... 18:41...

Melvin strode across the hangar floor, his posture straightening with each step despite years of captivity. The combat droids parted before him, their programming still recognizing his biometric signature as an authorized engineer.

"Still hiding behind machines, I see!" Melvin called out, his voice stronger than it had been in years.

Zoltar turned, genuine surprise flickering across his face before settling into smug amusement. He gestured, and his elite guards lowered their weapons slightly.

"Melvin Applebaum. Free of your neural dampener, I see." Zoltar's voice echoed across the hangar. "How does it feel to witness the fruition of our shared vision?"

"Our vision?" Melvin stopped in the center of the floor, surrounded by the machines he'd helped design. "We wanted to build protectors, Zoltar. Machines that would save lives, not enslave humanity."

Zoltar descended the platform via a sleek glass elevator, his exoskeleton whirring with each movement. "Such a limited perspective. You always were too sentimental for true innovation."

"Is that what you call this?" Melvin gestured at the rows of combat droids. "Perverting everything we worked for into weapons of oppression?"

"I call it evolution." Zoltar circled Melvin slowly, savoring the moment. "Humanity needs guidance, structure. My droids will provide both."

"You've twisted every design I ever created," Melvin's voice rose, drawing all attention in the hangar. "The adaptive learning systems meant to help people—you've weaponized them. The protective protocols—corrupted for control."

"Improved them," Zoltar corrected, tapping his cane against the floor. "Your designs were brilliant but purposeless. I gave them meaning."

"You gave them cruelty." Melvin's eyes flashed with anger. "That stabilization matrix wasn't meant for neural suppression. The kinetic dampeners weren't designed to incapacitate civilians."

Zoltar laughed, a cold sound that echoed through the hangar. "Such moral outrage from the man who built the most efficient combat robots the tournament had ever seen. Did you think those designs wouldn't have military applications?"

"I built them to test the limits of what machines could do," Melvin countered, his voice carrying to every corner of the facility. "Not to replace human choice with mechanical obedience."

Billy stared at the complex circuitry, paralyzed by doubt. Then he heard his father's voice echoing through the hangar—strong, defiant, buying him precious seconds.

"Come on," he whispered to himself. "Dad believes in you. They all do."

Zippy chirped encouragingly, extending multiple interface probes into the control panel. The drone's optical sensors pulsed rapidly as it scanned the security architecture, identifying backdoors and vulnerabilities with remarkable speed.

"That's it, Zippy!' Billy's confidence returned as his small friend navigated the system. "Find the authentication bypass."

The hub's display flashed a series of warnings, but Zippy countered each one, spoofing security credentials faster than the system could reject them. A progress bar appeared on Zippy's interface: 43%... 62%... 89%...

"Almost there," Billy murmured, fingers hovering over the physical controls.

Zippy emitted a triumphant beep as the final firewall collapsed. ACCESS GRANTED flashed across the panel, revealing the hub's core functions.

"Now for the power grid," Billy muttered, scanning the exposed circuitry.

He identified the main power conduits—thick cables pulsing with energy that fed into the quantum synchronization matrix. Unlike the digital security, this required physical intervention. Billy pulled tools from his belt, quickly disconnecting safety limiters and rerouting power flow patterns.

"If we overload the primary buffer..." He twisted two cables together, bypassing the surge protector. "And reverse the polarity here..."

The hub's cooling systems whined in protest as energy began to build up in circuits never designed to handle such loads. Warning lights flashed across the control panel.

SYSTEM INSTABILITY DETECTED.

EMERGENCY SHUTDOWN INITIATED.

OVERRIDE ATTEMPT DETECTED.

Zippy inserted itself deeper into the system, blocking the automatic failsafes with a continuous stream of override commands.

"Just a little more," Billy urged, connecting the final bypass.

The hub's blue glow intensified, shifting toward white as power surged through unregulated pathways. Throughout the hangar, the first row of combat droids twitched, their synchronized movements becoming erratic as conflicting commands flooded their processors.

"It's working!" Billy exclaimed as the chain reaction spread.

The quantum entanglement that linked the droids began to collapse, each machine's programming corrupting as the hub's signals degraded. Some froze in place, others jerked spasmodically, and a few simply powered down, collapsing like puppets with cut strings.

A high-pitched whine emanated from the hub as its systems approached critical failure. The countdown timer on the display flickered, numbers jumping randomly before freezing completely.

The node pulsed with unstable energy, its blue glow intensifying to blinding white. Circuits sparked and components melted as the quantum buffer reached critical overload.

"Get down!" Billy yelled, diving behind a maintenance panel and pulling Zippy with him.

The synchronization hub exploded in a deafening blast of light and sound. The shockwave rippled outward, hitting the first row of combat droids like a physical force. They toppled backward into the ranks behind them, systems shorting out in cascading waves across the hangar floor.

Hundreds of war machines collapsed simultaneously, their lights flickering and dying as the central control signal dissolved into chaos. The droids fell like dominoes —some freezing mid-step, others crumpling to their knees before powering down completely.

"No!" Zoltar screamed, his voice barely audible above the cacophony of failing machinery. "Override! Manual activation sequence!"

But his commands fell on deaf circuits. Without the synchronization hub, his army was nothing but metal and wires.

The victory was short-lived. A deep, ominous rumble vibrated through the floor as the hangar's structural supports began to fail. The explosion had compromised key load-bearing columns, and the ceiling groaned under its own weight.

"The place is coming down!" Relson shouted, dodging a falling support beam.

Massive chunks of concrete crashed onto the droid formation, crushing the inert machines. Dust filled the air as fissures spread across the ceiling in spiderweb patterns.

Melvin sprinted toward Billy's position as metal walkways twisted and collapsed around them. "We need to move! Now!"

Billy scrambled over debris, Zippy hovering protectively at his shoulder. They reunited with Cristen and Relson near what had been the main entrance—now blocked by tons of fallen concrete.

"The emergency exit?" Cristen coughed through the thickening dust.

"Sealed automatically when the systems failed," Melvin explained, scanning the crumbling hangar. "We're trapped."

Another section of ceiling gave way, forcing them back toward the center of the room. They huddled together as the space around them continued to collapse, the wreckage of Zoltar's army becoming their prison.

CHAPTER 21: OUT OF THE ASHES

A support beam crashed ten feet to Billy's left, sending concrete shrapnel flying through the air. He ducked, shielding his face as dust billowed around them.

"Move!" Melvin grabbed Billy's shoulder, yanking him sideways as another section of ceiling collapsed where they'd been standing seconds before.

The hangar transformed into a death trap—steel beams twisted like paper, electrical cables snapped and showered sparks across the wreckage, and the relentless groan of failing metal filled their ears. The remains of Zoltar's army became obstacles in their desperate flight, fallen droids blocking potential escape routes.

"There!" Cristen pointed toward a maintenance corridor barely visible through the chaos. "Service tunnel!"

They sprinted across the unstable floor, dodging falling debris. A massive ceiling panel crashed behind Relson, missing him by inches. He stumbled forward, caught by Melvin before he could fall.

"Watch out!" Billy shouted as a lighting fixture plummeted from above.

They scattered, regrouping on the other side of a fallen droid. The air grew thick with concrete dust, turning visibility to near zero. Zippy's lights cut through the haze, illuminating a path forward.

"Follow Zippy!" Billy choked through the dust.

The little robot zipped ahead, leading them through the labyrinth of destruction. A secondary explosion somewhere behind them sent a shock wave rippling through the hangar, accelerating the collapse.

Melvin pulled Billy under a partially fallen beam as rubble rained down. "Keep moving! Don't stop!"

They reached the maintenance corridor entrance, only to find it partially blocked by debris. Relson braced himself against the frame and pushed a fallen panel aside, creating just enough space to squeeze through.

"Go!" he grunted, muscles straining to hold the weight.

Cristen went first, followed by Zippy. Billy hesitated.

"I'm not leaving without you!"

"Nobody's getting left," Melvin promised, shoving Billy through the gap before turning back to help Relson.

The ceiling directly above them gave way with a thunderous crack. Melvin lunged forward, tackling Relson through the opening as tons of concrete crashed down behind them, sealing the entrance completely.

The narrow maintenance corridor offered momentary shelter from the collapsing hangar, but their reprieve lasted mere seconds. A deafening mechanical whine pierced through the rumble of falling debris, followed by the unmistakable hiss of hydraulics engaging.

"He's still coming," Melvin whispered, his face draining of color.

The far wall of the corridor exploded inward, showering them with fragments of metal and concrete. Through the dust emerged a towering silhouette—a sleek, midnight-black mech suit with glowing crimson accents. Its proportions were humanoid but exaggerated, standing twelve feet tall with armored plating that gleamed despite the dust and chaos.

"Is that—" Billy started.

"Guardian Prime," Melvin finished, voice hollow. "My final design. The prototype I never completed."

The mech's faceplate slid open, revealing Zoltar's gaunt face twisted in rage. "Leaving so soon, Applebaum? After I've spent years perfecting your creation?"

The suit's massive arms ended in articulated hands that could crush steel. Zoltar flexed them experimentally, the joints whirring with precision.

"You always lacked vision," Zoltar continued, advancing with thunderous steps that shook the corridor. "Guardian Prime was meant to be a masterpiece, not some tournament toy."

Melvin pushed Billy behind him. "Run. All of you."

"Dad, no—"

"Your precious family reunion ends here," Zoltar snarled, the mech's systems humming as weapons systems engaged. Shoulder-mounted missile pods rotated into position while the suit's forearm panels slid back to reveal pulse cannons.

Cristen grabbed Billy's arm. "We need to move!"

"Not without my father!"

Zippy darted forward, scanning the mech's configuration and beeping frantically.

"Zippy says there's a cooling system vulnerability at the back of the neck joint," Billy translated, eyes darting between his father and the advancing behemoth.

Zoltar laughed, the sound amplified through the mech's external speakers. "Your little toy can't help you now."

The mech lunged forward with unexpected speed, arm extended to grab Melvin. The corridor trembled under its weight as the group scattered, barely avoiding the attack.

"Split up!" Melvin shouted. "He can only chase one of us!"

"Get to the service elevator at the end of the corridor!" Melvin shouted, eyes locked on the mech suit. "I'll buy you time!"

Billy froze. "Dad, no—"

"I designed this thing, Billy. I know how to slow it down." Melvin's voice softened for a split second. "Trust me, son."

Cristen pulled Billy backward as Relson covered their retreat. Zippy hovered uncertainly between them.

"Zippy, go with them!" Melvin commanded, never taking his eyes off Zoltar. "Billy needs you!"

The little drone chirped in protest but followed as the group backed away.

Melvin reached into his pocket and pulled out a small device—a remote override he'd swiped from the medical bay. His fingers danced across its surface, inputting a sequence from memory.

"You forget, Zoltar," Melvin called out, circling to draw the mech's attention away from the retreating group, "Guardian Prime was built with my fail-safes."

Zoltar's face contorted with rage. "Failsafes I removed years ago!"

"Not all of them." Melvin ducked as the mech swung a massive arm, the hydraulics hissing. "The tertiary cooling bypass still requires manual authentication every ninety seconds."

He pressed a final button on the device. The mech's shoulder-mounted weapons suddenly locked up, the missile pods freezing mid-rotation with a mechanical groan. Zoltar howled in frustration, pounding controls inside the cockpit.

"And the pulse cannons still have the same overheating issue I never solved," Melvin continued, backing away as Zoltar redirected power to the suit's arms. "Thirty seconds of continuous operation, then a mandatory cooldown."

The mech lurched forward, its movements becoming jerky as auxiliary systems fought to compensate for the locked weapons. Melvin narrowly avoided being crushed against the wall, rolling beneath a wild swing and coming up behind the suit.

"The neck joint!" Billy shouted from down the corridor. "Dad, hit the cooling port!"

Melvin spotted the small ventilation grille at the back of the mech's neck—exactly where he'd designed it years ago. He grabbed a piece of broken conduit from the floor and jammed it into the port as Zoltar tried to turn.

Steam erupted from the joint as coolant lines ruptured. Warning lights flashed across the mech's exterior as its systems began emergency shutdown procedures.

"You'll pay for this, Applebaum!" Zoltar screamed, the mech's movements growing increasingly erratic.

"Go!" Melvin shouted to the others. "It won't hold him for long!"

Billy stopped dead in his tracks, watching his father struggle against the towering mech. The service elevator was just ahead—safety, escape, survival. Cristen tugged at his arm.

"Billy, come on! We need to go now!"

But something had changed in him. The fear that had always driven him to hide behind his inventions, to keep people at arm's length, to solve problems alone—it was still there, but it no longer controlled him.

"I'm not leaving him." Billy's voice was steady, resolute. He pulled his arm from Cristen's grasp. "Not again."

"Are you crazy?" Relson shouted. "That thing will crush

you!"

"Then it crushes both of us." Billy turned to Zippy, who hovered anxiously beside him. "Zippy, I need a distraction. Can you overload your power cell? Just enough for a flash, not an explosion."

The drone chirped affirmatively, its lights blinking in understanding.

"Billy, please—" Cristen began.

"He's my father." Billy met her eyes, no longer hiding behind his goggles. "I spent thirteen years wondering what happened to him. I'm not losing him again when I just got him back."

Before they could stop him, Billy sprinted back toward the battle, Zippy zooming ahead. The little drone positioned itself near Zoltar's field of vision and began to glow, its power cell charging beyond normal parameters.

"Dad!" Billy called out. "On my signal, drop and roll left!"

Melvin's head snapped toward his son, eyes widening in horror and pride. "Billy, no! Get out of here!"

"Now, Zippy!"

The drone released a blinding flash that filled the corridor with harsh white light. Zoltar screamed, the mech suit stumbling backward as its optical sensors overloaded. Melvin dropped and rolled as instructed, narrowly avoiding a wild swing from the disoriented machine.

Billy slid under the mech's legs, grabbing his father's hand and pulling him toward a maintenance alcove as the suit crashed against the wall, trying to recalibrate.

"I told you to run!" Melvin shouted, but there was no real anger in his voice.

"Yeah, well," Billy grinned, helping his father to his feet, "I guess I'm stubborn. Must get it from somewhere."

"The cooling system will reboot in thirty seconds," Melvin

whispered, his eyes darting between the staggering mech and the unstable ceiling above. "We need to move."

Billy scanned the corridor, his mind racing. "Look at those support beams—they're barely holding."

The maintenance alcove shielded them momentarily as Zoltar's mech regained its balance, optical sensors flickering back online. The suit's hydraulics hissed as it turned in a slow arc, searching.

"Come out, come out," Zoltar's voice echoed through the corridor. "You've only delayed the inevitable."

Melvin gripped Billy's shoulder. "The eastern section—it's already compromised. If we can get him under those main supports..."

"We'd need bait," Billy said, his gaze fixed on the weakened ceiling struts.

"I'll do it," Melvin started, but Billy shook his head.

"Together." He pointed to a half-collapsed archway twenty yards down the corridor. "That section is barely standing. One good hit from something his size..."

Zippy chirped softly, hovering near Billy's ear with a suggestion.

"Perfect," Billy nodded. "Zippy can remote-activate the remaining power cells from the fallen droids. The explosion would be enough."

The mech took a thunderous step toward their hiding spot, its sensors narrowing in on their location. They had seconds at most.

"On three," Melvin whispered. "One..."

"Two..." Billy's hand found his father's, squeezing once. "Three!"

They burst from the alcove, sprinting toward the compromised section. Zoltar's laugh boomed through the mech's speakers as he gave chase, the suit's massive feet leaving cracks in the floor with each step.

"Zippy, now!" Billy shouted.

The drone shot ahead, interfacing with a fallen combat droid's exposed circuitry. A cascade of sparks erupted as Zippy rerouted power to the droid's emergency systems.

"Keep moving!" Melvin pulled Billy forward as Zoltar closed the distance behind them.

They reached the archway, diving through just as the mech suit lunged for them. Its massive arm punched through the weakened wall, sending concrete fragments flying.

"Is that all?" Zoltar taunted, the mech tearing through the remaining structure to reach them.

Zippy completed the override. The fallen droid's power cell surged, then detonated with a concussive blast that shook the entire corridor. The explosion wasn't massive, but it struck precisely where the support structure was weakest.

A terrible groaning sound filled the air as tons of concrete and steel shifted above them. Zoltar looked up just as the ceiling began to give way, massive chunks of debris raining down on the mech suit.

The mech suit convulsed under the crushing weight of concrete and twisted metal, its limbs twitching with failing hydraulics. Warning lights flashed across its surface as emergency protocols engaged, the once-formidable machine now reduced to a pinned giant.

"We got him!" Billy shouted, coughing through the dust cloud that filled the corridor.

Melvin pulled his son back as another section of ceiling collapsed, widening the gap between them and the buried mech. "Don't celebrate yet."

A mechanical hiss cut through the rumble of settling

debris. The cockpit of Guardian Prime cracked open, its emergency release deploying despite the damage. Through the widening gap, they glimpsed movement.

"No," Melvin whispered, his face paling.

Zoltar emerged from the crushed cockpit, blood streaming from a gash on his forehead. His once-pristine clothes were torn and dust-covered, but his eyes burned with undiminished fury. He pulled himself free of the wreckage with surprising agility for his age, augmented limbs whirring beneath his clothing.

"You think this ends here?" Zoltar's voice was ragged but carried clearly through the settling dust. "You've destroyed nothing but a prototype!"

He stood atop the ruined mech, silhouetted against emergency lights that still flickered in the corridor. Blood dripped from his fingertips, but his posture remained unnaturally straight, defiant.

"I've had contingencies in place for decades, Applebaum!" He fixed his gaze on Melvin, then shifted to Billy. "Like father, like son—both of you too shortsighted to see the bigger picture."

Billy stepped forward, but Melvin held him back. Zoltar reached into his jacket, extracting a small device that glowed with an eerie blue light.

"We'll meet again," Zoltar promised, his finger hovering over the device. "And next time, I'll take everything you love."

He pressed the button. A blinding flash erupted around him, followed by a localized electromagnetic pulse that knocked out the remaining lights. When their vision cleared, Zoltar was gone, a small service hatch hanging open where he had stood moments before.

"He's gone," Billy breathed, staring at the empty space.

"For now," Melvin replied grimly, pulling Billy toward the exit where Cristen and Relson waited. "But we need to move. This whole place is coming down."

The group sprinted through the crumbling corridor, chunks of ceiling raining down around them. Melvin led the way, pulling Billy along while Zippy darted ahead, lights flashing to illuminate their escape route.

"There!" Melvin pointed to a narrow maintenance hatch set low in the wall. "Service tunnel! It leads to the outer perimeter!"

Relson reached it first, wrenching the rusted handle with both hands. The metal groaned in protest before giving way with a sharp crack. "Got it!"

A deafening rumble shook the facility as the hangar's main support beams finally gave way. The floor beneath them buckled, cracks spreading like lightning across the concrete.

"Inside, now!" Melvin shouted.

Cristen dove through the opening first, followed by Relson. Zippy zipped in after them, chirping frantically. Billy hesitated, looking back at the destruction swallowing Zoltar's life work.

"Billy, move!" Melvin shoved his son through the hatch before diving in himself, pulling the heavy door shut just as the corridor ceiling collapsed completely.

Darkness enveloped them, broken only by Zippy's dim emergency lights. The thunderous roar of the collapsing facility surrounded them, the walls of their narrow sanctuary vibrating with each new collapse. Dust filtered through tiny cracks in the tunnel, filling their lungs and stinging their eyes.

"Everyone okay?" Melvin coughed, his voice barely audible over the continuing destruction.

"Still breathing," Relson wheezed, helping Cristen to her feet.

Billy pressed his ear against the sealed hatch. "It's all coming down. The whole hangar... all those droids..."

"Buried," Melvin confirmed, placing a hand on Billy's shoulder. "That army won't threaten anyone now."

The final, massive crash reverberated through the tunnel, so powerful it knocked them off balance. Then, gradually, the rumbling subsided, replaced by an eerie silence broken only by the settling of debris and their ragged breathing.

"We did it," Billy whispered, the reality of their narrow escape sinking in. "We actually did it."

Zippy hovered near the ceiling of the cramped tunnel, illuminating the dust-covered faces of the group. Despite exhaustion and injuries, a cautious sense of triumph passed between them.

* * *

Melvin led them through the winding service tunnel, his movements confident despite years of captivity. The path sloped gradually upward, carrying them away from the destruction below.

"Almost there," he whispered, voice hoarse from dust and emotion. "Fresh air ahead."

A faint glow appeared at the tunnel's end—not artificial light, but the warm orange of sunset. They quickened their pace, drawn to it like moths.

Relson reached the exit first, pushing aside a rusted grate that had been hidden behind decorative shrubs outside the arena's eastern wall. He tumbled out onto soft grass, laughing with exhausted relief as he rolled onto his back.

"We made it," Cristen gasped, emerging next. She reached back to help Billy, who pulled Zippy through after him.

Finally, Melvin stepped into the fading daylight, blinking at the open sky—the first time he'd seen it unfiltered in years. He stood motionless, face tilted upward, tears cutting clean tracks through the grime on his cheeks.

Billy watched his father, too overwhelmed to speak. The moment felt fragile, sacred.

A crowd had gathered beyond the security perimeter, held back by confused guards who had no idea what had happened inside. The ground trembled with aftershocks as more sections of the underground facility collapsed.

"Not bad for a bunch of scrapyard kids."

The gravelly voice came from behind a maintenance shed. Juno Kett stepped into view, his disguise abandoned. He'd reverted to his familiar wild appearance —beard beginning to return, clothes rumpled and stained.

"Caveman!" Billy exclaimed. "How did you—"

"Slipped away when the guards rushed inside." Juno grinned, wiping blood from a split lip. "Figured you might need an escape route cleared."

He gestured toward a service vehicle parked nearby, its Zoltar Industries logo hastily painted over. "Transportation, courtesy of our mutual friend."

Melvin stared at Juno, recognition dawning. "Kett? Juno Kett? The champion who disappeared?"

Juno nodded, extending a calloused hand. "And you're the legend they locked away. Seems we both found our way back to the world."

A roar erupted from beyond the security barriers as the crowd surged forward. On the massive arena screens—originally designed to broadcast tournament battles—chaotic footage played of Zoltar's secret facility collapsing, intercut with images of Billy and his team escaping.

"Look at the screens," Cristen whispered, pointing upward.

Zippy chirped excitedly, spinning in circles above their heads.

"That's my doing," Juno said with a wink. "Found the broadcast controls while you were underground. Thought people deserved to see the truth."

The screens showed Zoltar's combat droids, hundreds of them, now buried beneath rubble. Then footage of Melvin confronting Zoltar, his voice somehow captured: "You twisted everything we built into weapons!"

The crowd's cheers grew louder. Security guards looked at each other uncertainly, then stepped aside as people pushed through barricades.

"It's them!" someone shouted. "The ones who stopped Zoltar!"

A wave of spectators surrounded them, hands reaching out to touch their shoulders, their arms. Children pointed at Zippy, who preened under the attention. Reporters shoved microphones forward, questions overlapping into unintelligible noise.

"Heroes!"

"How did you know?"

"Are those Zoltar's war machines?"

"Was he planning an attack?"

Billy shrank back against his father, overwhelmed by the crush of bodies and voices. Melvin's arm tightened protectively around him.

"Didn't exactly plan on becoming public figures," Relson muttered, though he couldn't hide his smile as a group of teenagers chanted his name.

An older woman pushed through the crowd, tears

streaming down her weathered face. She clasped Melvin's free hand between both of hers.

"My son worked for Zoltar. Disappeared three years ago. We never knew..." Her voice broke. "Thank you. Thank you for exposing him."

Others joined her, sharing similar stories of missing loved ones, of suspicions ignored by authorities. What had begun as celebration transformed into something deeper—a collective catharsis, years of fear and uncertainty finally validated.

Cristen found Billy's hand and squeezed it. "You did this," she whispered. "You brought them answers."

Billy looked around at the faces—grateful, relieved, hopeful—and for once, didn't hide behind his goggles.

The crowd eventually parted, creating a small island of calm around Billy and his father. Melvin placed both hands on Billy's shoulders, taking in the sight of his son —no longer the small child he remembered, but a young man who had risked everything to find him.

"Look at you," Melvin whispered, voice cracking. "Your mother always said you'd grow up to be twice the engineer I was. She was right."

Billy swallowed hard, fighting the lump in his throat. "I just wanted to find you. I didn't know if—"

"I know." Melvin pulled him into a tight embrace. The years of separation dissolved in that moment— the emptiness that had haunted Billy's childhood, the questions that kept him awake at night, the void that no amount of tinkering could fill.

"Mom never gave up," Billy murmured into his father's shoulder. "She kept everything exactly as you left it. Your workshop, your tools..."

Melvin pulled back, eyes glistening. "Rebecca. How is

she?"

"Waiting. Always waiting." Billy smiled through tears. "She's gonna flip when she sees you."

Zippy circled them, chirping excitedly.

"And this little marvel," Melvin laughed, looking up at the drone. "Your creation?"

"From your spare parts. He understands me better than most people."

"That's the Applebaum touch." Melvin ruffled Billy's hair. "We build things that connect, not just function."

The setting sun cast long shadows across the arena grounds. In the distance, emergency vehicles arrived to secure the collapsed facility, but here, in this moment, there was only father and son, standing beneath an open sky that seemed endless with possibility.

"Let's go home," Melvin said softly. "I've missed enough of your life already."

Billy nodded, unable to speak past the emotion tightening his chest. Together, they turned toward Juno's waiting vehicle, arms still around each other's shoulders—the beginning of a journey back to the life they should have had, to the woman who had kept faith through all the silent years.

CHAPTER 22: HOMECOMING

Juno's repurposed cargo hauler rumbled through the streets of Biome Synthesis, its suspension groaning under the weight of its passengers and the salvaged parts of The Reckoner they'd managed to retrieve. The city around them pulsed with energy unlike anything Billy had ever seen.

"Look at that," Cristen said, pointing at a massive holographic display stretched across the living wall of the Central District. It showed footage of the arena collapse, with "ZOLTAR EXPOSED" flashing in bold letters.

People filled the streets, clustering around public screens, their faces illuminated by the blue glow of emergency broadcasts. Some cheered as the hauler passed, recognizing its occupants.

"Word travels fast," Melvin murmured, his face half-hidden in shadow as he gazed out at the city he hadn't seen in years. "Everything's changed."

They crossed from the gleaming Central District into the Temperate Ring, where engineered oak trees formed living archways over the roadway. News drones buzzed overhead, their cameras tracking the hauler's progress.

"City authorities have confirmed the arrest of twelve high-ranking officials connected to Zoltar's operation," announced a voice from a nearby public address

THE ADVENTURES OF: BILLY BOLTS

system. "Meanwhile, search teams continue to assess the underground facility where an estimated five hundred combat droids were discovered..."

Billy leaned against his father, still unable to believe he was real, solid, alive. "Mom doesn't know we're coming. I couldn't risk contacting her."

"Better that way," Juno said from the driver's seat. "Zoltar might have associates monitoring communications."

Relson, who had been uncharacteristically quiet, suddenly laughed. "Look at that!" He pointed to a makeshift banner hanging between two biofuel stations: "SOUTHERN DISTRICT HEROES" painted in bold strokes.

"They spelled my name wrong," Cristen groaned, but she was smiling.

As they entered the Southern District, the hauler slowed to navigate the narrower streets. Here, the celebrations were more intimate—neighbors sharing stories on doorsteps, children reenacting battles with toy robots, street vendors giving away food to mark the occasion.

"Never thought I'd see the day," an old man called out as they passed. "Zoltar's been stealing our brightest minds for decades!"

Zippy zoomed ahead, scouting their path, occasionally returning to circle the hauler with excited chirps.

"Almost home,' Billy whispered, his heart pounding as they turned onto the familiar street where his mother waited, still unaware that her family was finally whole again.

The hauler stopped in front of the modest home with its small front garden of drought-resistant succulents. Billy jumped out before the engine fully powered down, his heart hammering against his ribs.

"Mom's gonna..." His voice caught. "She's not expecting..."

Melvin stood beside him, suddenly hesitant. "Does she—did she ever—"

"She never stopped believing," Billy said. "Never."

The front door opened before they reached it. Billy's mother appeared, wiping her hands on a kitchen towel, her expression shifting from curiosity to disbelief as she registered the group approaching her home.

"Billy? What's going on? I saw the news about the arena, and I was worried sick—"

Her words died as Melvin stepped forward into the porch light. The kitchen towel slipped from her fingers. For a moment, she stood frozen, one hand rising to cover her mouth.

"Mel?" The word escaped as barely a whisper. "Is it really —"

"It's me, Rebecca." Melvin's voice cracked. "Our boy found me."

She took one uncertain step forward, then another. Her hands reached out, trembling, touching Melvin's face as if to confirm he wasn't a hologram or a dream. Then her knees buckled.

Melvin caught her as she collapsed into his arms, her body shaking with sobs that seemed to come from somewhere deep and long-sealed. His arms enveloped her completely, his face buried in her hair, murmuring words only she could hear.

"Twelve years," she managed between gasps. "Twelve years, I knew you were alive."

Billy stood watching, his own vision blurring with tears. Cristen's hand slipped into his, squeezing gently.

"You did it," she whispered.

His parents sank to their knees on the front path, still locked in their embrace, decades of separation dissolving in tears and broken sentences. His mother's hands moved frantically over Melvin's face, shoulders, arms—as if cataloging changes, confirming reality.

"They said you were dead," she sobbed. "But I knew. I always knew."

Melvin looked up at Billy over his mother's shoulder, his face streaked with tears. He extended one arm, and Billy stepped forward, joining the embrace as the family circle closed at last.

As the family embraced on the front path, a small crowd began to gather. Neighbors emerged from their homes, drawn by the commotion and whispered news spreading through the Southern District like wildfire.

Old Man Jenkins, who'd spent forty years salvaging tech from the district's scrap heaps, shuffled forward with his hover-cart piled high with gleaming metal components. His weathered face crinkled into a smile beneath his gray stubble.

"Applebaum," he called out, addressing Melvin. "I thought you were gone for good. Should've known any father of Billy's would be too stubborn to stay captured."

Rebecca wiped her eyes and turned, still keeping one hand firmly on Melvin's arm as if afraid he might disappear again.

Jenkins gestured to his cart. "Been saving these servo-joints and power couplings for something special. Guess bringing down Zoltar's whole operation qualifies." He nodded at Billy. "Your boy's been rummaging through my yard since he could walk. Figured I'd save him some trips."

More neighbors approached, some carrying food, others with salvaged tech parts. Mrs. Patel from three doors down brought a steaming tray of samosas. "For the heroes," she insisted, pressing it into Cristen's hands.

"My cousin worked in the Eastern District assembly plant," called out a young woman Billy recognized from the market. "Zoltar's people took him five years ago. Search teams found him and thirty others in the lower levels today."

The Rodriguez twins, mechanical engineers who ran the district's best repair shop, pushed forward with a crate of pristine tools. "For rebuilding," they said simply, nodding at Melvin with professional respect.

"We watched the tournament feeds," said Mr. Chen, the retired transport pilot. "Knew something was wrong with Zoltar's operation for years, but nobody could prove it. You kids did what the authorities couldn't."

Jenkins cleared his throat. "Southern District looks after its own. Always has." He gestured at his cart of parts. "These are yours. And there's more where that came from. Whatever you need to rebuild."

The gathering had grown to nearly thirty people, a small crowd forming a protective circle around the reunited family and their friends. Not just neighbors, but a community that understood exactly what had been lost—and found.

As the impromptu neighborhood celebration continued into the evening, Juno stood slightly apart from the crowd, watching the scene with quiet contemplation. His cleaned-up appearance still felt strange after years in the caves, but something had shifted in him since meeting Billy and joining their mission.

He approached the Applebaum family, who were still surrounded by well-wishers. When there was finally a break in the conversation, he cleared his throat.

"I've been thinking," Juno said, his voice carrying an unusual certainty. "About what comes next."

Billy looked up, suddenly concerned. "You're not going back to the caves, are you?"

Juno shook his head. "No. That chapter's closed." He gestured toward the gathered neighbors and their contributions. "Seeing all this—a community that builds rather than destroys—it reminds me why I became an engineer in the first place."

Melvin nodded in understanding, one arm still around Rebecca's shoulders.

"I'm going to start a workshop," Juno continued. "For kids like you, Billy. Young engineers who need guidance, not competition." He smiled slightly. "Figure I've got some knowledge worth passing on, and too many years wasted hiding from the world."

"That's... amazing," Billy said, genuine surprise in his voice.

"You showed me something important," Juno said, meeting Billy's eyes directly. "That brilliance without purpose is just waste. And fear without action is just another prison." He glanced at Relson and Cristen. "And that the right team makes impossible things possible."

He extended his hand to Melvin, who grasped it firmly. "Your son's quite something, Applebaum. Reminds me of you—but better."

Melvin laughed. "No argument there."

Juno nodded respectfully to Rebecca, then turned to leave. At the edge of the gathering, he paused and looked back at Billy.

"Drop by the workshop sometime. I'll be in the Eastern District, near the old factory complex. Might need a consultant with your particular talents."

With that, the former Caveman walked away, his posture straighter than it had been in years, purpose evident in every step.

As the neighborhood celebration began to wind down, Billy found himself sitting on the front steps of his home, watching as Relson demonstrated his improvised EMP disruptor to a group of wide-eyed district kids. The night air carried the mingled scents of Mrs. Patel's spices and the earthy aroma of the district's living walls.

Cristen appeared beside him, holding something wrapped in a scrap of blue cloth. She settled next to him, their shoulders touching.

"You've been quiet," she said.

Billy nodded. "Still processing, I guess. Everything happened so fast."

Inside the house, he could see his parents through the window, his mother's hands moving animatedly as she talked, his father listening with an expression of wonder, as if he couldn't believe he was home.

"I have something for you." Cristen placed the cloth-wrapped object in his hands. "Salvaged it from what was left of The Reckoner."

Billy unwrapped it carefully. Inside was a small component—the neural interface they'd designed together, the part that had connected pilot to machine. Its casing was scratched but intact, the intricate circuitry visible through a transparent panel. She'd cleaned it, repaired the damaged connections, and added a small hook so it could be worn as a pendant.

"It was the heart of everything," she said quietly. "The part that made The Reckoner more than just metal and wires."

Billy ran his thumb over the interface, feeling the familiar contours. "You fixed it."

"Some things are worth saving, even when they're broken." She nudged his shoulder with hers. "Thought you might want to keep it. To remember."

"Like I could forget." Billy's voice caught slightly. "Thank you. For this, and... everything else. For believing in me when I didn't."

Cristen smiled, the expression softening her usually serious face. "That's what friends do. We see each other clearly, even when we can't see ourselves."

Billy looped the cord around his neck, the interface resting against his chest—a small, tangible reminder of what they'd built together, what they'd overcome.

"Unbreakable," he said, tapping the component. "Like us."

The neighborhood gathering had thinned as evening deepened into night. Under the soft glow of bioluminescent garden lights, Billy stood examining the broken components they'd salvaged from The Reckoner. Each piece told part of their story—dented armor plates from the arena battles, scorched circuit boards from the final confrontation with Zoltar.

A shadow fell across the parts, and Billy looked up to find Relson standing awkwardly before him, hands shoved deep in his pockets. The usual swagger was gone from his posture.

"Hey," Relson said, shifting his weight from one foot to the other. "Got a minute?"

Billy nodded, setting aside a damaged power coupling.

"I've been thinking," Relson began, then stopped, frustrated with his own hesitation. "Look, I was a real jerk to you. For years." He gestured vaguely toward the scrap yard in the distance. "All that time I spent pushing you around, calling you names..."

"Water under the bridge," Billy said, but Relson shook his head.

"No, it's not that simple." He pulled something from

his pocket—a small, crudely welded figurine made from scrap metal. "Made this while you were talking with your folks. It's supposed to be Zippy. Not great, but..."

Billy took the figurine, turning it over in his hands. Despite its rough appearance, there was genuine care in the details.

"I was scared," Relson admitted, his voice dropping. "Scared I wasn't smart enough, wasn't good enough. Easier to tear others down than build something myself." He looked directly at Billy. "I'm done with that. The bullying, the tough guy act—all of it."

Billy remained silent, watching the transformation happening before him.

"Whatever you build next—whatever crazy invention you come up with—I want in." Relson's expression was earnest, vulnerable. "Not as the muscle. As part of the team. I want to learn how to make things better, not break them."

Billy extended his hand. "Deal. But fair warning—my next project involves repurposing obsolete water filtration systems. Not exactly combat robots."

Relson grasped his hand firmly, a genuine smile replacing his usual smirk. "Even better."

As the night deepened, the neighbors gradually returned to their homes, leaving the Applebaum family to process their reunion in private. Billy sat with his father in the workshop that had been sealed for so many years, surrounded by half-finished inventions covered in dust—relics of a life interrupted.

Melvin ran his fingers over an old blueprint, tracing the faded lines. "I designed these to protect people," he said quietly. "Zoltar twisted everything—took defensive systems and repurposed them for conquest."

Billy nodded, understanding now why his father's creations had felt familiar yet wrong in Zoltar's hangar. "That's why The Reckoner worked so well. It wasn't built to attack—it was built to defend."

"You saw what I couldn't," Melvin said, placing a hand on Billy's shoulder. "I got lost in the possibilities of what technology could do. You understood what it should do."

Outside, the first hints of dawn lightened the sky. Through the workshop's small window, they could see Rebecca moving around the kitchen, preparing breakfast as if determined to make this first morning together perfect.

"I'm never leaving again, Billy." Melvin's voice was firm, resolute. "Not you, not your mother, not this home we've built. Whatever comes next, we face it together."

Billy picked up one of his father's old welding tools, feeling its weight, its purpose. "I want to build things that matter," he said. "Not for tournaments or glory—but to protect people, to make their lives better." He looked up at his father. "Like you tried to do."

"That's the true purpose of invention," Melvin agreed. "Not what can be built, but what should be built."

Billy nodded, his expression solemn but determined. "I promise to use everything I've learned—everything you've taught me—to protect, not destroy." He gestured to the workshop around them. "This is our legacy. Not weapons, but solutions."

Melvin pulled his son into a tight embrace. "You've already surpassed me," he whispered. "I couldn't be prouder of the engineer—and the man—you're becoming."

The evening air carried the sweet scent of night-blooming jasmine from the Biome Synthesis gardens.

JASON M APPLETON

Billy, Melvin, and Rebecca sat on the rooftop terrace of their home, a space that had once been Rebecca's solitary refuge during long, lonely nights. Now, it held all three of them beneath a vast canvas of stars.

Rebecca had brought up a faded quilt, wrapping it around their shoulders against the gentle chill. Billy nestled between his parents, their familiar warmth on either side of him. The physical reality of their presence— his mother's soft breathing, his father's solid shoulder— anchored him in a moment that still felt dreamlike.

"I used to bring you up here when you were tiny," Rebecca said, smoothing Billy's hair. "You'd fall asleep counting stars while I told you stories about your father building robots that could touch the sky."

Melvin chuckled. "Not quite the sky, but close enough."

Billy leaned back, gazing at the constellations. The Southern District's minimal light pollution made the stars exceptionally clear, patterns of light stretching into infinity. He felt small beneath them, yet somehow complete in a way he'd never experienced before.

"What happens tomorrow?" Billy asked, his voice quiet in the stillness.

Melvin's arm tightened around him. "Tomorrow we start rebuilding. Not just machines, but everything."

"One day at a time," Rebecca added, her fingers finding Melvin's across Billy's shoulders, completing the circle.

Billy closed his eyes, absorbing the sensation of being held between them—the missing peace restored, the circuit completed. For years, he'd filled the emptiness with machines, with motion, with the constant whir of invention. Now, in the stillness, he found a different kind of wholeness.

"I always thought finding Dad would be the end of the

246

story," Billy murmured. "But it's just the beginning, isn't it?"

His parents didn't answer with words. Instead, they drew closer, the three of them gazing upward as a meteor streaked across the night sky—a brief, brilliant moment of light against the darkness, a promise written in the stars.